additional praise for

WE ARE A TEEMING WILDERNESS

I loved entering Shena McAuliffe's curious and elegant worlds, portrayed precisely and lovingly in these pages. The familiar slips into the strange, the past morphs into another universe entirely, and I could have lived in any of these stories forever.

—ANTON DISCLAFANI
author of *The After Party: A Novel*

Shena McAuliffe is not so much the author or the composer of these textured and tectonic fictions as she is the arranger, the conductor, the maestro taking single songs and scoring each into idiosyncratic symphonies. *We Are a Teeming Wilderness* is all about soothing cacophonies of jangled juxtapositions, foils and foiling sheets of story like the folds that make the edge of a katana, idiomatic sawdust turned into stardust into the dust of dust. Each story is its own archeology, a dig into texts, a kind of fruitful and fulfilling destruction, a concoction of simple machines, fragmented vessels, bejeweled fossils. What a glorious midden! What inhabitable follies! What restored and restoried ruins!

—MICHAEL MARTONE
author of *Plain Air: Sketches from Winesburg, Indiana*

We Are a Teeming Wilderness

Also by Shena McAuliffe

Glass, Light, Electricity: Essays

The Good Echo: A Novel

WE ARE A TEEMING WILDERNESS

winner of the press 53 award for short fiction

SHENA MCAULIFFE

Press 53
—•—
Winston-Salem

Press 53, LLC
PO Box 30314
Winston-Salem, NC 27301

First Edition

Cover design by Claire V. Foxx

Cover art: "Cross-section Plant Stem under the microscope
for classroom education. stock photo" by Sinhyu. Licensed
with permission through iStock.

Library of Congress Control Number
2023932003

ISBN 978-1-950413-61-4 (softcover)
ISBN 978-1-950413-62-1 (hardcover)

For all my teachers

CONTENTS

REAL SILK

House to house, and at every door a stranger. Trimmed lawns and flagstones. Orange trees and sprawling live oaks. The hedges and trees were much neater than in Ruben's own neighborhood. Bungalows with river-rock pillars and wide, shady porches. Bathrooms with tiny towels and seashell soaps and lavender water. And the ladies—there were some beautiful ones.

This one with black hair piled on her head—a mess, but she was wearing lipstick anyway. She had a smudge of something on her nose. It looked like engine oil. Maybe she was cleaning the oven. Ruben was suddenly shy, an expensive luxury for a salesman. But then there were the women with acne, and those with bad breath, with Cream of Wheat dribbled and crusted on their blouses. But all of them had legs, wore stockings, had a pocketbook and a pen.

Ruben was responsible for selling stockings to every woman east of Orange Grove, between Colorado Street and California Avenue. He had thick brown hair and a new pair of glasses—a splurge paid for with tips from the bread delivery job he'd quit in April when William offered him the Real Silk route. He lived with his mother on the other side of the Suicide Bridge, near the Linda Vista Hills. On bad days he thought of the people who had fallen or thrown themselves from the edge into the arroyo—the way they must have looked as they plummeted. Did they kick or flip? Flail their arms? Seem to float? But usually he just looked at the curve of the bridge high along the bank, the way the sun set the concrete aglow.

We wouldn't open our doors to him. Not nowadays. What, with robbers roving the cul-de-sacs? The rapists in police uniforms? With even the kids selling candy for The Boys and Girls Club pocketing your dollars for themselves? Put your eye to the peephole. Drag the barking schnauzer to the bathroom.

But it was hard for Ruben, too. He was a stranger at the door, puffed up like a rooster. Like an ex-con: suited and combed, shoes gleaming. He stood on the latch side, hidden until the door was mostly open. Two and a quarter feet from the threshold, intimate, but not intimidating. He flashed the button on his lapel. An official emissary from Real Silk Incorporated. A Real Silker. A door-to-door.

- *Smile. Step forward slightly.*
- *Say, "How do you do" (not Howdy-do).*
- *Avoid talking like a parrot. Speak conversationally, as one human being to another.*
- *If she tries to close the door, the situation will require backbone.*
- *Transferring the Advance Letter to the left hand, raise the right hand with the forefinger extended, and say dominatingly, but still SMILING—"Just a minute, madam."*
- *Properly done, this will halt her retreat nine times out of ten.*
- *Say, "Don't you want to know how to prevent runs in silk hosiery?"*

There were so many of them. An army of salesmen, with polished buckles and cases stuffed with stockings or chicken breasts. Or hawking vacuum cleaners, leather shoes for the mister, gilt-edged family Bibles, miracle solvents, electric irons.

Women were more often home. Maybe they were bored. Maybe they were seething. Pinning the diaper on the clothesline. Pinning the diaper on the baby. Sometimes they came to the door with their hair in their eyes. Take this one, holding the door with her hip, pushing a baby into his arms. Babies liked to blow little bubbles, to paint his glasses with soggy zwieback. Babies had sharp fingernails. They were all arms and legs and fat to Ruben. They smelled a little sour, or they smelled like talcum, the smell of his mother's bathroom. The clean ones he didn't mind. Their mothers chewing gum, hitching their skirts, bending down to buckle a shoe.

read first:

The Automobile never attained general popularity until the Self-Starter was invented.

From the beginning I have felt, and have repeatedly said, that the success—in fact, the very existence—of REAL SILK is dependent upon the prosperity of our representatives.

But I have long been seeking something that would do the same thing for us that the Self-Starter did for the Automobile business.

In this Sales Manual, developed as the fruit of several years' experience, by more than five thousand representatives, and codified for the first time at the 1923 convention:— *for the Real Silker*

I think we have at least what we have been seeking.

I hereby put myself on record, that if you, the representative, will work an honest eight hours per day, and WILL CONSCIENTIOUSLY FOLLOW EVERY INSTRUCTION IN THIS BOOK— *bold type reads*

IT WILL BE UTTERLY IMPOSSIBLE FOR YOU TO MAKE ANYTHING BUT A COMPLETE SUCCESS OF YOUR WORK.

That is why we call this an AUTOMATIC Sales Manual.

Mr. C. Kobin

◆ ◆ ◆

You may have failed in several other lines of work before you started with Real Silk, and yet you may still make a success of your life, if:
1. You find out and admit the cause of your previous failures.
2. You are willing to pay the price of success.
If you have not yet attained a really solid and fixed position in life, lay the blame squarely at your own door. Don't try to shift it to someone else.

Ruben had failed as a student, a paperboy, a sandwich maker, and a bread deliveryman. As a child, he had failed to clean his plate at every meal. He had failed to win a single footrace. Failed to regularly do his chores. Failed to save his father from death. Failed to comfort his mother over her loss. Failed to take his mother on holiday to Hawaii, on holiday to anywhere. Failed to fight for his country, to find a wife, to have a child or even a dog. His mother was rapidly losing her mind and he was failing to do anything to preserve it. He had failed to learn to sing, to cultivate a voice of butter and silver. Failed to make close friendships. Failed to write a play. Also, he was fat and had never been to the opera.

His mother used to call him "Rube" but never at temple and not in front of company. She stopped the practice entirely around the time she started getting careless with her makeup. She never called him Rube anymore. She rarely called him anything.

"Ma," he said, holding out a handkerchief. "Lipstick on your teeth."

She had always been meticulous—no stray hairs or clumped lashes—but still, he hadn't recognized the lipstick smears, or the single shadowed eyelid, as a symptom. She was only forty-nine. Too young for dementia, but the lipstick was only a portent, an augury of the iceberg's calving, its frigid bob and drift.

Ruben watched her sitting at the table, a cup of tea growing cold, a closed book beside it. Her steely hair needed a trim and frizzed around her face. She looked exhausted, the skin beneath her eyes thick and soft and slumping. Maybe that was it.

"You tired, Ma?" he asked. She didn't look up.

Then there was the way she often forgot words, took to gesturing midsentence, her cupped hand raised and circling as if the word might fall into it like a hailstone or a freshly laid egg.

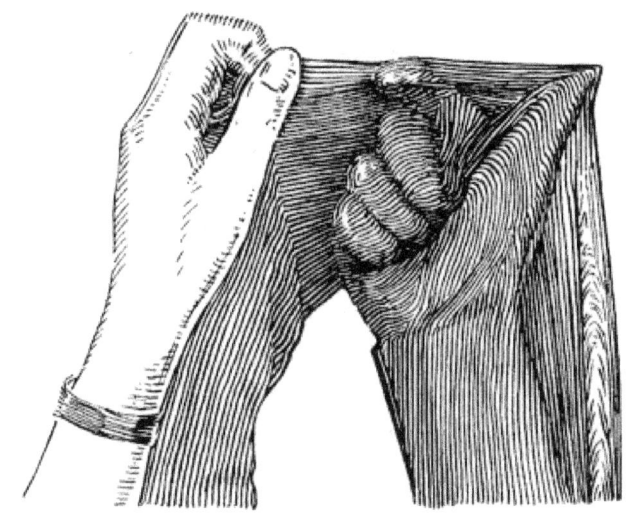

The Story of Silk

Every great industry has its romance. Whether it be that great section in western Pennsylvania, where steel mills darken skies and tell of prosperity, or whether it is the depth of a blackened mine—whether it be the spiring smokestack of the camera industry, the burning fires of thousands of coke ovens, or the countless acres of windblown grain—all these have their own individual romance, a story of human interest as their source, a spot where human beings dreamed and their dreams came true.

The silkworm crawls along a branch—tiny mandible gnashing, body plumping—gorging itself on mulberry leaves. The worm binds herself tight, spinning a corset from her own fibrous spit. She sleeps. She wakes. The acids of her body etch through her cocoon. She burrows her way out, unfurls her papery wings. So many leaves to produce this flitting, this batting at the lantern. The eggs she lays are the size of a pin's head and stuck to the underside of a leaf.

Ruben dreams of a silkworm farm: row upon row of mulberry trees, sunshapes shifting on the brown grass. Workers wander the orchard, stripping the leaves from each branch, filling baskets hanging from their arms. The hands float as if sewing, pulling thread through sky, leaf, and basket. The bare branches look like flayed fingerbones. The sun parches a new section of grass.

On the toilet, Ruben reads about the Silk Road from a new pamphlet William had given him. How it stretched its veins and vessels across Asia to Italy, where families slept in the stable, giving up the house so pupae could sleep on the pantry shelves, in the chifforobe, in the bed, or in the bathroom, all along the mantle. How women snuggled cocoons between their breasts, where the temperature was just right. The Silk Road boarded ships, and the silkworms sailed the ocean, hulls and holds stuffed with cocoons, which would soon be baked, or bathed in acid to kill the pupae before the moths destroyed the silk. And then the fibers were unwound, stretched, and washed, dried, dyed, and spooled, woven into ties, blouses, dresses, stockings.

But the real romance, Ruben thinks, is between his customer's leg and the stocking he hopes to sell her, which makes him a matchmaker. Ringing and knocking, smiling and proffering. A parrot alights in a nearby tree, chattering so loudly Ruben can't be heard, so the woman invites him in and leads him to the sitting room, offers him a cold glass of lemonade. Her skin, he tells her, can kiss the luxury of Ancient China. He drapes a sample over her wrist.

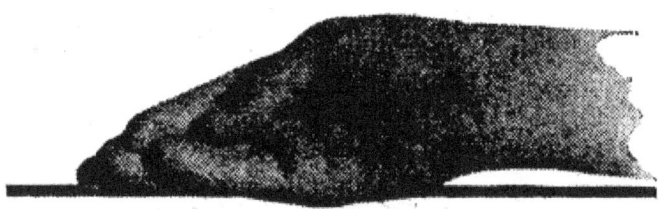

PHOTOGRAPH No. 4
Position of fingers as hand is put
into foot of stocking

If you are not by nature enthusiastic, cultivate an appearance of enthusiasm by imitating it, just as an actor would. If your imitation is any good it will react upon yourself, and you will soon be naturally enthusiastic. If you are not already enthusiastic and cannot acquire enthusiasm, you will never become a salesman or a REAL SILKER, and the sooner you know it, the better.

Ruben's sample case was covered with brown tweed and had nickel-plated spring-closure hasps. Nudge the buttons and—snap!—the lid opened, revealing an array of stocking samples pinned to a card. Navy, cordovan, black, white, nude, three different shades of gray; eight droopy silk toes aligned. They looked deflated at first, but if he set them on the table and angled them toward the light, the fibers gleamed, which seemed to revive them. Closing the case offered its own satisfaction and was almost as snappy, allowing for an abrupt exit if the sale had gone poorly, and made him feel brusque and powerful if the sale had gone well, and then he always made sure to throw in the free package of Ivory Soap Flakes.

The best thing in his case, and one of his best sales tools, was the silkworm cocoon that he used to tell the customer about how silk was produced. It looked a bit like a madeleine or a marshmallow, plump and soft and bready. It was creamy colored, with a few frizzy strands forming a pale cloud around it. He had cut the cocoon in half with a razor blade, and after a customer had studied it whole, he would open it, lifting the top half like the lid of a ring box, holding it on one flat palm, displaying the pupa, shining like a nut, dead and brittle on its nest of raw silk. The pupa was smooth, its brown body segmented like a pinecone, but its stunted wings were evident, tightly wrapped and shellacked, never to soften or unfurl.

He never let the women touch the pupa, but there he was, sitting alone in the back of the streetcar. He ran his finger over its segments and thought of the cartilage between his knees, the cracking of chicken bones. He apologized to the pupa under his breath but wasn't sure what he was apologizing for—that the worm had been sacrificed for silk stockings, cut short? That its silk had not even made it into stockings but was instead toted around in his case everywhere he went? That he revealed its fat, dead body to at least fifteen women a day, never letting it rest in peace? Or simply that he had touched it with his clumsy, slightly greasy finger?

The teakettle was wailing. It was belching like a smokestack, and his mother was nowhere to be found. That there was still water in the kettle seemed a good sign, but he found her in the yard, scuffling through the packed dirt, lightly touching the tops of the yuccas as if counting them. *Duck, duck, duck.* The full lungs. The waiting for *goose.* She wore one shoe and a winter coat (it was June).

She didn't answer when he called to her, so he walked across the yard, through the motes and haze. He touched her shoulder and found it unfamiliar, smaller than expected. It was as if he were approaching a stranger in the street, perhaps to tell her she had dropped something valuable—a train ticket or a watch or a pocketbook—and when she turned to face him, he saw that he was a stranger to her, too. They were actors, meeting on a sidewalk on a stage. Her eyes looked past him. She emitted a sound he couldn't classify—both scream and moan—a sound that picked up where the kettle had left off, its tone lingering in his ears when her lungs finally emptied. He pictured them—her lungs—out of air, front and back tissues clinging. She gasped and the lungs refilled. She looked at him.

"Did you get the bread?" she asked.

People have been losing it since they first staggered upright and dragged their fingertips through the mud, but perhaps it wasn't as evident back then, being easily interpreted as an evolutionary lapse into primitivism, the brain still shrugging its residual grunts, still feeding on raw meat and grubs plucked from the undersides of decaying logs.

Ventricles enlarging, opening, emptying.

Hollowing, hallowing. The demented move toward sainthood, tortured and visionary. Invisible sparks from neurons to dendrites are electrical messages, projected onto the internal movie screen, the mind's eye. But in the brain with dementia the nerves are snarled, a frayed and tangled mess. The messengers wander onto dead ends, into live wires, fizzling but leading nowhere. The messages get lost.

The stove is hot, says the neuron. Or: *This is your baby, all grown up. Don't you know him? Your own child? Your Rube?*

In the last presidential election, most Californians had voted for Calvin Coolidge, the incumbent, who won by a landslide. The average Californian could expect fifty-four years of life. A drive from New York took about thirteen days. The city of Pasadena was growing more slowly than during the last census period, but it was still growing by 54 percent. The Jewish temple was four years old. The trenches, the poison, the bayonets and tanks of the Great War, were six years in the past. The ashes, the bones, the pooling ink, the poisons of WWII, were fifteen years in the future. Four years had passed since Henry Ford published the first article in his series of four: "The International Jew: The World's Problem." Einstein's paper on special relativity had existed for nineteen years. Einstein himself was forty-five, half gray and bright-eyed, two years away from writing in a letter: "I, at any rate, am convinced that [God] does not throw dice."

If you could run alongside a beam of light, it would appear as a point in space, like the slowly spinning blade of a fan tracked by your retina, clearly defined, as if standing still.

It is difficult to imagine a world before the Holocaust, but light has been speeding for so long, shadows have been scarring the film for ages.

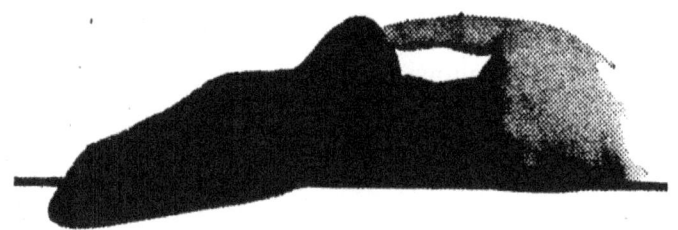

Photograph No. 5
Note the rounded heel

Genuine silk is an animal fiber, sensitive to heat, cold, friction and strain, and while it is the strongest and finest of all animal fibers, it is sensitive to improper handling. That is the keynote of your service education.

An animal fiber. Like skin or fur. Like muscles or tendons or eyeballs. Ruben decided against offering those parallels. "Like hair" would do. Think how carefully you must handle your hair. You wouldn't dye it with just anything. You wouldn't wash it with lye or bleach. You certainly wouldn't brush it with the potato scrubber.

Silk hosiery should be washed as quickly as possible after each wearing, never thrown in with the general wash. The stockings have absorbed, while worn, the waste matter (perspiration) which is constantly thrown off by the pores. The liquid acid in perspiration may evaporate, but if the hosiery is laid away soiled, part of the acid remains to attack the silk.

When Mrs. Helen Barney took off her shoe, and Ruben leaned toward her with the sample stocking, he smelled the clammy stink of her foot. She had been wearing shoes without socks. Her toenails were brittle and unpainted. He smelled her briny sweat, her laundry detergent, and something else—something like bread baking. Like her pillowcase would smell when she'd just risen and the cotton still held her heat. He couldn't help it—he took a deep breath and held it in his lungs, swished it like wine across his tongue.

There is a difference between courage and nerve. Courage is the quality that enables you to look the seventh prospect in the face and smile after you have been turned down by the six preceding prospects.

He rang and knocked at the same time. A bucktoothed blonde in a green dress opened the door. He had dropped off the advance letter the day before, so she knew he was coming.

"How do you do?" he said.

"I've got plenty of stockings, sir." She smiled and her teeth seemed even more prominent.

"Real Silk are not just any stockings, ma'am. May I show you some samples? I'm sure you'll be impressed."

She stopped smiling.

"I never buy from canvassers." She closed the door swiftly, no time for dominating smiles, no time for "madam."

He rang and knocked at the same time. No one came. He went around back. Knocked again. No one. He knocked again. He counted to one hundred. He wedged an advance letter in the door.

He rang and knocked at the same time. He stood on the imaginary X, feet shoulder-width apart, one hand on the button on his lapel, other hand ready for shaking. She cracked the door and couldn't see him, cracked it further.

"How do you do?" he said.

"You're the third peddler today," she said. "And it isn't even lunchtime." She closed the door.

He rang and knocked. Knocked and rang. Rang and knocked.

"I only wear lisle. Silk is just too fragile."

"No, no, I'm just not interested."

"I'm too busy today. Maybe come back another time."

"My husband doesn't allow me to talk with canvassers when he's out."

"I don't need any stockings, but can I have the soap flakes anyway?"

Pausing under a live oak, he wiped his forehead with the back of his hand. It was almost midday and even the birds were quiet. He shrugged his shoulders a few times to loosen them up. He practiced his smile—with teeth, without teeth.

He climbed the steps to a heavy-looking bungalow. A reel mower sat in the yard but the grass was yellow. His sample case pulled at his shoulder. He let it fall on the doorstep beside him. It rocked on its hasps. He rang and knocked.

She said, "Good morning."

"You remember me?" he said. "Mr. Gilmore of Real Silk. I left you a letter yesterday, which entitles you to our service, without cost or obligation. I have also been instructed to leave you a package of Ivory Soap Flakes. Have you read the letter?"

"Oh, my," she said, smoothing her hair over her ears. "Yes, yes."

He leaned down to pick up his case and felt his belly spilling over his waistband, pressing against the leather belt, the buttons and zips and buckles and fibers. Sweat rolled around from the back of his neck down the front of his shirt. He lifted the case. "I'll just step in, with your permission."

She stepped aside, holding the door wide so he could enter. He imagined the heat of his body bouncing off her cool skin, a heated frying pan meeting a half-frozen pork chop. The door clicked shut. He was supposed to lead her into the sitting room, get her seated and comfortable, get her chatting. But all the doors from the foyer to the rest of the house were closed. Where had she come from? It was like he had walked into in a closet. He put his case down.

Practice saying—"Mrs. Jones, here is one of the most interesting things you ever saw in your life," and when you have learned to say it with the right enthusiasm in your tones, and the right expression of complete sincerity in your face, you will never have any more trouble in showing the book.

A tiny woman wearing an embroidered apron and house shoes. A cap of hair that she continually smoothed, alternating hands. A voice that seemed to come from the bottom of a well.

"It's too dark here," he said. "Might we go where you'll be more comfortable?" He put his hand on the nearest knob. She didn't stop him, so he turned it and pushed the door open, once again lifting his case as he stepped into the living room. A rocking chair and a sofa faced off across the floorboards. Bare walls. No table. No lamp. No rug. It was even darker than it had been in the foyer.

"We keep the curtains closed so it doesn't get too hot." She fanned herself with her hand. "I just hate this heat."

He pushed the rocking chair closer to the sofa and tipped it forward for her. "Will you be so kind as to be seated? I want you to be comfortable, and what's more, when you sit down it's easy for me to show you this remarkable picture of our laboratory." She sat. Ruben listened to his own voice, echoing and stiff.

He opened the case. She watched him, her entire head tracking his movements like a cat watching a bird through a window. He exhaled. She would buy no more than a single pair of stockings—lisle, probably, which was practical, durable, and cheap—or she might order socks for her husband. He tried not to rush the presentation.

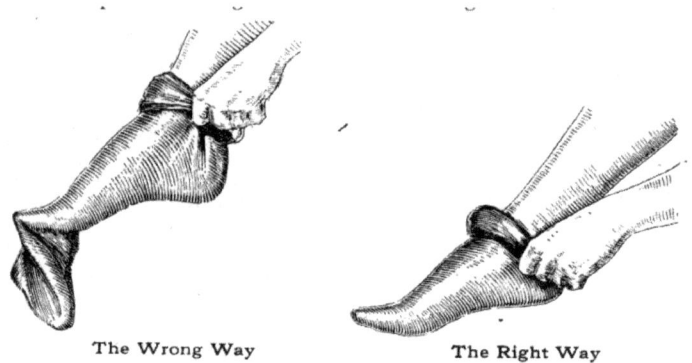

The Wrong Way   The Right Way

*The price of success is **effort**. Mental as well as physical. Thinking as well as doing. Driving yourself steadily forward to earn your ten dollars today—and then putting in some evening hours on the problem of how to earn eleven dollars tomorrow.*

Ruben had not broken eight dollars in three weeks. He had considered tagging along with William again, asking for more training, but that would mean no sales at all for that week. Ruben waited for William across from The Grand Opera House, a three-story brick-and-mortar building with arched stone windows that had thirty-six years to Ruben's thirty. It now housed the drugstore, where he and William ate their Wednesday lunches.

Ruben loved the opera house. Years ago it had been topped with onion domes, gilded and bronzed, and the stage was complete with a heavy curtain dropping between acts, but the opera goers had shivered in their cushioned seats, their bones rattling, their lips bluing in the balcony—it was unheated. By the time Ruben discovered opera, no voice had sung on that stage for years. It had been a stove and heating showroom, barely a hotel, and now the drugstore.

Standing across the street, at the post office, Ruben imagined the opera-goers hitching up their silks and feathers, gliding to their seats for a production of *Madame Butterfly*. Their need for stockings was tremendous. Their need for silk slippers. The tiny glasses they unfolded in the balcony, their eyelashes spidering against the lenses.

"Ahoy there, pal-ee!" William loped up the sidewalk, practically shouting. He was hatless, his blond hair shining. His tie hung loosely. "Don't know about you, but I'm sure ready for some grub."

A thing must be pictured in the mind before it is realized, so if you would appeal to a customer's imagination you must first get a clear image in your own mind of the picture you intend to paint for her. You may not have imagination naturally, but it can be cultivated.

Ruben sat at the kitchen table, cultivating his imagination, while, on the phonograph, Caruso sang the part of Pinkerton in *Madame Butterfly*. It was Ruben's favorite opera—the quiet passion, the privacy of Butterfly's death. And Pinkerton was such an obvious villain, a clear-cut cad, so undeserving of Butterfly's devotion. But despite the character he played, Caruso's voice was absolutely heroic. What woman could resist him? If only he, Ruben, could sing like that! From the other room an occasional snore cut through the music. His mother slept, her belly full of mashed potatoes, Ruben's specialty.

Indeed, it was difficult to imagine being a woman. He pictured Helen Barney, with her messy hair and the smudge on her nose. She had ordered a half dozen silk and a single pair of lisle—a decent customer. She kept her hands soft and smooth—no ragged callus or hangnail would ever snag her stockings. Ruben held his hands out and inspected them, but instead saw Helen's hairless knuckles, her nails gleaming with red enamel.

Ruben imagined Helen's husband sitting at their kitchen table in a cloud of smoke, puffing a fat cigar and reading the paper, drinking a whisky and water. The blue smoke softened the lines of the furniture and the wrinkles on his face but made Helen's eyes burn. Her husband ignored her, occasionally lifting his glass for a refill, seeing her only later, in the bedroom, when it was time to do his husbandly duties. His kisses would taste of whisky and tobacco.

What would make Helen, this soft-handed wife of a cigar-smoking whisky swiller, buy stockings? Would they recapture her husband's attention? Would they stave off the scaly dryness of age?

He tried to imagine—closed his eyes even—but on the phonograph Cio-Cio San had reached the moment of her suicide and Ruben was distracted. In his mind, Helen became Cio-Cio San. Her need for silk stockings, and her husband and his cloud of smoke, all drifted off. All Cio-Cio San wanted was an honorable death. She stood with her dagger poised, her blindfolded child on the floor at her feet.

Ruben pushed his chair back from the table and stood. He sang along with the opera, his voice cracking. He raised his own imaginary dagger to his chest. *Oh, for love!* The dagger fell. He plunged it and then collapsed onto the table, spilling a glass of water. A fork clattered onto the floor.

PHOTOGRAPH NO. 6
**The way to put stocking
on forearm**

♦ ♦ ♦

No matter how good a salesman you are, you are going to lose a certain percentage of orders if you do not keep yourself neat and clean. Your clothes do not have to be expensive, and they ought to be quiet and conservative, but they must be kept freshly pressed and brushed. Linen should be spotless, and shoes shined. Be careful of your teeth and fingernails.

He stood with one hand extended, the advance letter slightly creased between his thumb and forefinger. The other hand held his hat, tipped slightly toward her, shielding his heart. The woman wouldn't take the letter.

"My letter of introduction," he said again. He shook the letter a little.

She narrowed her eyes and slowly, deliberately, looked him up and down. He straightened up, re-tipped his hat.

"What did you say your name was again?" she asked.

"Gilmore, ma'am. Ruben Gilmore."

She nodded. "Gilmore. Yes. Well, I have no interest in your goods, Mr. Gilmore."

"I'm a service man, madam, sent by Real Silk to help you get better results from your hosiery. There's no obligation to buy anything." With his hat, he touched the button on his lapel to show her he was bona fide.

"I am just not interested in anything you're selling." She stepped back into the house and slammed the door.

Ruben stared at the anchor-shaped knocker. The advance letter rattled in his outstretched hand.

He turned and walked down the drive, where a Ford was parked. He slapped the car's taillight as he passed. Slapped it hard. Then he spit on the tire. He paused to watch the spit roll down the gleaming hubcap. He spit again.

A stocking or sock should never be pulled on by grasping it at the top and forcing the foot down through the narrow ankle. The stocking should be rolled up in the hand clear down to the heel—slipped over the toes and then unrolled evenly and smoothly until first the foot and then the entire stocking is fitted. That's the right way and the easiest, too.

William had hired Ruben and trained him, but they knew each other from the deli, where William had been a regular customer (pastrami on rye, extra mustard, no pickle). William was a top Real Silker—fair and blond and friendly. He had square, white teeth.

"Take a look at this," William said, beckoning Ruben to lean in. They were sitting side by side at the counter. William usually spent lunch swiveling his stool, an inch this way, two inches back, but he was perfectly still now, holding something in his lap.

Ruben set his sandwich on the plate. Mouth full of egg salad, he leaned close to William. Under the counter, William held a small tin box. The label was orange and showed the silhouette of an Arab on a horse, wrapped in billowing cloth, the words "Three Sheik" in blue lettering over his head.

"Condoms," William whispered. "The ladies *love* this brand. Something about the horseman. They go nuts." He cracked the tin so Ruben could see the rubber coins resting in the box.

"I don't use them," Ruben whispered, feeling the heat rise to his cheeks. He licked a bit of celery from the corner of his mouth. William raised an eyebrow, winked, and tucked the tin back into his pocket.

"You can get them here," he said. "Right up front. On the way out."

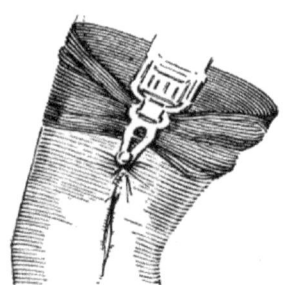
The Wrong Way

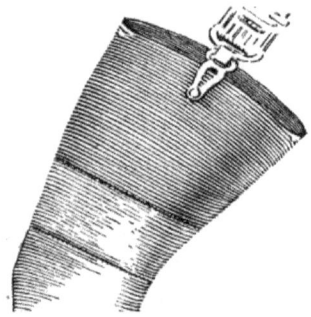
The Right Way

Ruben took a huge bite of his sandwich and chewed slowly.

Ruben's mother had been almost beautiful, but there was something off about her chin. It was too pointy, too small. Plus, she was shy. She rarely laughed. She always looked away. There had been a time when her body filled her clothes, weighting and pushing at the fabric, but lately her bathrobe seemed empty and electric, rippling with static. Once, when he was helping her to bed, she had flung the robe off her shoulders with no warning, letting it fall to the floor, and she stood there in only a sagging pair of underpants. He rushed from the sight of her small breasts, hitting the light switch in time to see the blue sparks still leaping and crackling in the robe around her ankles.

His father, too, had been hunched and shriveled. While other fathers strode jauntily along the sidewalks, off to their jobs in fedoras and suspenders, Ruben's dad tripped over his shoelaces, spilled his tea, scattered toast crumbs down his shirt, wiped his nose with the back of his hand. He was sick by the time Ruben was twelve, beset by a constant cough, all kinds of rattling and running. His voice all but disappeared, as if it had slipped down his throat and gotten lost among the terrible organs. Ruben brought him things while he sat in his chair. The newspaper. His slippers. His dad patted him on the head as if he were a dog.

Be persistent. The surest success-rule in closing is to make a woman say NO three times before you give up. Women rarely mean NO the first time they say it.

Helen opened the door. She was smiling. Her face was clean, scrubbed-looking and pale. Her hair was combed and parted, pulled back tightly, but the second button on her dress was missing, and she was barefoot.

"Well, Mr. Gilmore," she said.

"Just checking up," he said. "I happened to be on your street. Has your order arrived?"

"Come in, come in." She held the door for him and stepped to the side.

He went in and set down his case. She put out her hand for his hat, which she hung on a rack with three other hats. She saw him looking.

"My husband insists on different shades and different colored feathers," she said. She took a gray one down and showed him the feather—dappled black-and-white with a blue tip.

"Very nice," said Ruben.

"He could keep the haberdasher in business all by himself." She put the hat back. "Would you like some tea? Or something cool? I think we have cream soda."

A baby began to cry.

"I'll be right back," she said. "Go on in and sit down, Mr. Gilmore."

He went into the sitting room, where he had sold her the stockings, and settled on the sofa. He leaned back and flung his arm over the back of the cushions, imagining Helen next to him. She came in holding the baby and sat down on the sofa, not quite under his arm. Blushing, he folded his hands in his lap and sat up straight.

"This is Millie," she said, shifting the baby around so he could see.

"Hello, kid." He winked at the baby, who gurgled and rammed her head into her mother's neck. "So have your stockings arrived?"

"Not yet. But it's only been a few days," she said. The baby whimpered a few times and then wailed. "Didn't you say it would take ten?" She bounced the baby up and down.

"Yes. They're coming all the way from Indiana, you know."

The baby screamed.

"I should go," he said, but he didn't move.

"I have to feed her," Helen said. "Do you mind?"

He gave a nod.

She unbuttoned the front of her dress. What was she doing? Only poor people breastfed their babies. He looked away but couldn't help it—he looked back.

"I really should get going," he said again. The baby had latched onto Helen's breast. It was a mollusk. He couldn't move.

"Are you married, Mr. Gilmore?" she asked. She had pulled the edge of her dress so it covered everything the baby's face did not, but the smooth skin above her breast, above the baby, was bare. Her skin was so pale. She did not look strong enough to feed another living creature. He could see the blue of her veins, the faint shadows where her ribs met her sternum. There was a mole, just off center, round and black, a single spot on a die, a terrible roll.

"No," he stammered. "I live with my mother."

"Oh," she said. "I hope my little Millie here will take care of me like that someday. If I need her to." Millie detached herself and Ruben saw Helen's nipple, wet and pink. The baby smacked her lips and gasped, then reattached, gulping furiously. That the creature would grow up, become a person—a woman—it was impossible. Millie flailed and grabbed at her mother. Ruben could not look away.

Then he was touching Helen's knee, laying his hand on it. His hand was a monster. He stared at it. His fingernails were immaculate. Helen didn't move. His fingers were spread, crawling over the edge of her thigh. She sighed and the baby clucked. She sighed again, then straightened up, shifting away from him. He pulled his hand back.

"Mr. Gilmore," she said. "I'm really sorry. You should go."

No matter toothpaste, astringents, or soaps. No matter vitamins and unguents, blueberries or green tea. The body is a traitor. It stretches and dapples. Rattles and oozes and gasps and heaves. Neurons dive into wormholes. The brain is so easily tricked: a magnetic field is goodness, is god, is hovering, is a ghost, is an epileptic seizure. The left hand loses track. The right hand takes another cookie and another. The pancreas defects. The white blood cells divide and divide.

◆◆◆

*I trust that you now have a clear conception of the
raw product of which our stockings are made. The
story of silk is interesting. The kiddies will like to hear
it. Grownups, too, enjoy the tale. There is nothing but
pleasure in telling the story of Real Silk.*

He stood on the sidewalk, blinking in the three o'clock
sun. The row of houses sat sealed against him, holding
their breath, full of hats and plates and socks. Across
the street he saw another salesman—brown fedora,
tweed case—stepping out of a house, loudly thanking an
unseen customer. The man walked down the driveway,
nodded to Ruben, walked on to the next house.

They were an army. A squadron in suits and shiny
shoes, with balding heads and swinging sample cases. He
pictured them as from above, tracking their footprints
up and down the street, crisscrossing each other's paths,
marching over each other's shadows. Up and down the
walkways. A tipped hat, a nod, knocking on the same
doors, one after another. Bells rung. Brass rings lifted
and tapped. Doors opening and closing. Silk stockings.
Radiators. Life insurance. Light bulbs.

From his pocket he took a stack of advance letters
and let them slide from his hand into Helen's yard. It was
a windless day. He kicked at them, then mashed them
with his foot. Parrots yammered in the trees.

*"Ivory Flakes" are absolutely pure—contain no alkali or
harsh ingredients—and make such an abundance of suds
that harmful rubbing is unnecessary. Proved ideal for
washing silk hosiery, by laboratory tests, we recommend
their use exclusively.*

"Ma!" he called, closing the door.

The house was too hot. He set his case down and
took off his shoes, setting them side by side on the mat.
He could hear her somewhere in the house—creaking
floorboards, shuffling feet. "Ma!" he said again. She

wasn't in the kitchen. He heard water running some-where.

He found her in the laundry room, in front of the sink, tap gushing. Steam and suds spilled onto the floor, piling around her ankles, mingling with a dozen torn and crumpled Ivory packets.

"Ma!" He crossed the room and shut the water off, feeling his socks grow instantly wet. "What are you doing?"

She had a scrub brush in her hand—a small one, with fine white bristles, the kind meant for cleaning mushrooms or tomatoes or lace. Over her other hand she wore a navy stocking, stretched up to her elbow. Fingers spread, hand rigid, she was scrubbing hard. The silk was a mess of snags. Her skin was raw and scalded. When he turned the water off she looked at him, slowly.

"Hello, dear." She sighed.

He took her hands and turned the cold water on, maneuvering her hands under the faucet. He soaked a cloth and pressed it to her skin.

"Well, that's very nice, dear," she said.

A bubble floated by and she puckered her lips. She blew it toward him like a kiss.

DISPATCHES FROM ABANDONED ARCHITECTURE

1.

There used to be many singing cowboys. This was before my time, and I tend to mix them up, especially Roy Rogers and Will Rogers, who are unrelated and separated by years, one vaudeville and the other radio. When I rocked in a chair on the porch of the Will Rogers Ranch, it was Roy I was thinking of. His Pop built a houseboat of salvage wood and floated the family up the river, but the river flooded, so they scooted the boat to shore, where it dried like horse bones in the sun. The boy who would one day be Roy Rogers lined up rocks in the dirt, smallest to largest, and yodeled at them. In the grass, the grazing cows were thin and milkless.

2.

In his most attractive years, Will Rogers had hair like yours: dark and glossy with an unruly part. And like you, he looked smashing in black with pearl snaps. He, too, was narrow-waisted, and his charm became goofy with age. You used to sing to the cat, to the coffee, to my hair, which was mashed and electric from the pillow. On a January morning, we went out early to sled on the hill beside the cemetery, and you rode a snow horse we found, a snow horse that someone else had built, a sweatshirt for your saddle. When you leaned into your ride, it did not matter that the horse was made of snow, that the sky was slate gray, that the city down the hill, in the wide valley, seemed suspended in toxic smog. It mattered only that we had a sled and a wild horse on which to ride.

3.

Once, I wiped the lipstick from my teeth with a tissue, and you snapped your pearl snaps all the way up, and we went out for a night on the town. But now, if I stand to the east, I can see the blue of the ocean through the plastic and scaffolding. When the workers hung the tarps, they meant only to scrape paint without getting wet, but when I sit in a rocker under the limbs of the old trees and watch the sun through the bones and skin of their setup, the blurred cliff on the other side becomes a chorus of cowboys riding.

4.

In the night, a train whistle sometimes sounds like a harmonica, and the shaking windows murmur. Sometimes, it is a brass chord swelling warmly in the dark. Sometimes, it is butterscotch pudding. But other nights, it is pots and pans hurried into the low cabinet, a winter night that falls too soon. Sometimes, it is headlights through the trees, casting shadows through the tent. The Doppler yaw, the rattling windows, empty bottles flung against the rocks.

5.

The horse bones in the dry grass were not much like the arched scaffolding of Jonah's whale, but I thought of Jonah nonetheless, resting in his quiet cavern in the sea. Spoon of the collarbone, piano-key spine, locusts hurdling their airy hotel. I held a rib against the sky, the ocean its wet opposite.

6.

When I stop wearing a pair of shoes, their holes stretch. The stitches come loose more quickly. The soles curl. I find them in the closet full of dust and dead box elder bugs. This happens to houses, too. As if the warmth of human bodies were the mortar between the bricks, that which kept the pigeons out of the rafters. In the empty house, pages blow one to the next, unturned by human hands. Something always burns. Look carefully. Dig next to the splintered rocking chairs and chipped flowerpots. You might find the dried collarbone of a horse, a spice jar buried with a plastic army man inside, a bit of satin fringe, a pearl snap from a cuff.

THIS PRECARIOUS HIVE:
DENTURE HOUSE AT THE
MUSEUM OF MODERN ART

During summer of 2011, two unemployed graduate students were hired by the Elizabeth Cutler Haven House to care for the elderly of Salt Lake City, Utah. Natalie Carson and Luisa Moulton spooned Jell-O cubes and creamed corn into so many mouths. They changed sheets and pushed wheelchairs, led games of charades and singalongs. But while the elderly slept, Carson and Moulton stole their teeth for the sake of art.

Denture House[1], the third collaborative work of the artist duo Natalie Carson and Luisa Moulton, is a six-foot tower of dentures and other dental material the artists stole from the residents of Elizabeth Cutler Haven House, an assisted living home where they worked from June 2011 through January 2012. It is the first of their collaborations to explicitly take the form of Art (with a capital A), and their first sculpture. Their preceding collaborations were ephemeral, spontaneous

---

[1] Natalie Carson and Luisa Moulton. 2012. Dentures (acrylic resin, silicone, porcelain), dental crowns and bridges (alloy, ceramic, leucite), teeth, epoxy.

"performances" that went largely undocumented and left no permanent artifacts.[2]

Carson and Moulton worked at the Elizabeth Cutler Haven House for fewer than seven months, but in that time they managed to acquire seventy-two pairs of dentures and an assortment of crowns and bridges. The sculpture includes four gold and seven ceramic crowns, four dental bridges, and fourteen natural teeth, many with extensive decay indicating they probably fell freely from resident mouths or were removed by dentists. It is unclear whether the women acquired these pieces by coercion, natural "shedding" on the part of their charges, or manual removal. The artists claim that all the teeth were given freely or stolen when residents had removed them from their mouths for cleaning or sleep. If the teeth were taken

---

[2] Potentially apocryphal: when questioned, the artists refused to discuss such "juvenilia."

First, Carson and Moulton gathered a "bouquet" of 500 flowers from various gardens in Natalie Carson's neighborhood and left them on the doorstep of Esther Shafak, a friend who corroborates the story in *ARTnews* (May 2013): "There were lots of tulips, some daffodils, and a lot of things I couldn't name heaped on my doormat. I couldn't get past them. The ones on the bottom of the pile were already turning brown and the entire hallway smelled sweet and rotten. It must have taken them hours, and they left the neighborhood gardens looking a little bald. There were actually bees hovering around the flowers. . . . I say there were 500 because that's what Luisa said when she confessed that she and Nat had were behind it. She told me a week or so later, after having denied responsibility at least three other times. . . . No, I don't think it was a joke but rather that they meant to do something nice for me. It was a gift. . . . She said they started stealing flowers from gardens, and after they'd gathered about a hundred they set a goal for what they thought would be really excessive, and then they counted aloud as they picked."

In the second reported project, Carson and Moulton filled diffuser air fresheners with urine. ("Diffuser" air fresheners are jars filled with scented oil. "Sticks" are inserted into them like flowers in a vase. These sticks, which look like incense, absorb the scent and disperse it into the air around them.) The artists distributed jars to the restrooms of two local cafes where Carson had previously been employed (and quit) and to a bakery where Moulton had been employed (and fired—reasons unknown).

while the residents were sleeping, the victims must have been out cold to sleep through the removal of even their most rotten tooth. When speculating along these lines, it's necessary to consider that the sound sleep was due to pharmaceutical aids administered by the women. While this is pure conjecture, it must be noted that Carson had a prescription for Eszopiclone (Lunesta), which she refilled regularly. When arrested, she also had a partly used package of Nyquil gel caps in her purse. After Carson and Moulton were arrested for larceny, police found dental tools in Moulton's residence, but Carson and Moulton have consistently denied charges of such foul play, and as only one resident of the E.C.H.H. has ever posited such a claim—a man in his nineties who suffered severe dementia and is now deceased—no charges have ever been pressed.

The dentures and other accoutrements balance on and in each other, affixed with epoxy, which is neither acid-free nor archival, but since dentures are designed to dwell for as long as possible within the corrosive chemistry of saliva, the sculpture is projected to have extensive longevity. Dust is its greatest enemy.

The artists dubbed the sculpture a "house,"[3] though the interior cavities do not appear as dwelling spaces for anything larger than a bumblebee. In fact, the sculpture appears hive-like in its intricacy and repetition. In a 2013 interview with local news and gossip monthly *S.L.U.T.* (*Salt Lake's Ultimate Tattler*) Carson stated that she and Moulton may have been subconsciously influenced by the culture and icons of their community. About half the population of Salt Lake City belongs to the Church of

---

[3] House. Home. Dwelling place. Refuge. What makes one? Narrow painted clapboard and tomato plants? Textiles and five different light sources per room? An affectionate pet? A well-stocked refrigerator, including olives, whole milk, and blueberry Stilton? But a cave could make a lovely home, with a few burning candles and five or six books stacked next to a pillow stuffed with the soft fibers of cattails. A coastline. Rainy winters. Rusted warehouses. Twilights that turn high green leaves golden.

Jesus Christ of Latter-Day Saints[4] (LDS, or "Mormons"
in vernacular, though some find this label derogatory).
In 1844, church leader Brigham Young designated the
beehive as the symbol of the church and eventually of
Salt Lake City and the state of Utah.[5] There are beehives
everywhere: on manhole covers, on the state flag, capping
stairway banisters, and even, occasionally, as the focal
point of some fabulous tattoo.[6] In the same 2013 interview,
Moulton professed some confusion over the symbol:
   "Everybody knows a hive is run by a queen. All the
drones, which are asexual, are at her command. Brigham
Young had eighty wives—he was most definitely the
queen bee—but it seems the church confused the gender
roles. Brigham Young was not effeminate. And his wives
weren't asexual, at least not as far as I can tell. And they
sure had a lot of kids. The Mormon church is incredibly
patriarchal, but a beehive is the ultimate matriarchy."[7]
   Why the artists chose to steal dentures has never been
clear; even during their trial, they failed to explain. Carson and
Moulton plead guilty and were convicted of theft in winter
of 2014. They did time in low-security prison (Carson was

[4] Although the percentage of LDS members along the Wasatch Front
is far higher, the percentage of believers within the city proper dipped
below 50 percent for the first time in 2004 and has continued to
decline. This "urban decline," however, is somewhat misleading as the
LDS church is the fastest-growing faith in the world, and in the state
of Utah, LDS members make up over 60 percent of the population.

[5] The state motto is "Industry"—busy little bees.

[6] The LDS church, it should be noted, states on its website that
"Latter-day prophets strongly discourage the tattooing of the
body. Those who disregard this counsel show a lack of respect for
themselves and for God." These beehive tattoos must, then, adorn
the skins of rebels and nonbelievers, indicating that the symbol has
transcended its religious roots and become an emblem of local pride,
ironic or otherwise.

[7] Ginger Tanner. "Artist Duo Arrested for Denture Theft." *S.L.U.T.*,
June 15-22, 2013.

imprisoned for two years, Moulton for eighteen months.)[8] By
the time the court reached a verdict, many of the E.C.H.H.
residents whose teeth had gone missing were dead, and few of
those who were still living wanted their teeth back. During her
testimony, Moulton confessed that the artists often stole the
dentures of deceased residents. When preparing a body for
funeral services (if there was to be an open casket viewing),
the mortuary employees often assumed the person had mis-
placed his or her dentures during the fading days of life. Occasionally, a set of loaner dentures was fitted into the deceased's
mouth for the viewing, their lips pressed closed to disguise
the mismatched teeth. "The wrong pair of dentures makes a
familiar face look remarkably strange, changing the person's
appearance to a degree that makes them unrecognizable,"
says Carlton Ensign, Director of Ensign Funeral Home in Salt
Lake City.[9] These loaner teeth were often removed before
burial or cremation, unless the loved one's beliefs stipulated
that the body would be restored as-is in the afterlife, in which
case the loved one would need whatever teeth he or she could
get[10] in order to chew the beef and sugarplums of eternity.

---

[8] Time in prison proved remarkably productive for the collaborators.
They completed and planned multiple works, including the much-
lauded toilet-papier-mâché cast of Moulton's biceps (*Prison Biceps*,
2014. Toilet paper, water, flour) and the associative map of the
Stewart Low-Security Prison (*Hive Map*, 2014, graphite on paper).

[9] Carlton Ensign. Telephone Interview. November 12, 2014.

[10] Being Platonic, most Christian denominations believe the body
will be restored to its "most perfect" state during rapture, that God
will correct any challenges the body faced in its earthly life. The
lame shall walk; the bipolar shall exalt without ever swinging back to
weeping and lamentation, etc. By this system, no one will need a set
of crappy dentures in the afterlife; every body will be will reborn with
a set of straight white teeth. This raises questions far more complex
than the writer is prepared to address in this article: Will there be
bodies in the afterlife? Will there be *time?* And *ages?* And what would
be the most perfect age for the body? Will every person be the same
ideal age, with adult teeth, perfect muscle tone, taut gleaming skin?
(*How dull is heaven?*)

Of the denture-theft victims still alive at the time of the artists' arrest, many were pleased to be part of an artwork that would outlast them. Some families initially appalled at learning their loved one had been robbed of teeth or dentures eventually bragged. "Who would do such a thing? Steal dentures? It's just disgusting," said Ericka Roundy, daughter of former E.C.H.H. resident Kenneth Roundy, whose dentures are included in the sculpture. "At first we were angry, but Dad was dead by then. Honestly, Dad would think the whole thing pretty hilarious. I mean, it's super creepy, and those women are definitely sick, but we have no need for Dad's teeth. And the piece is in New York now, at MOMA, which is pretty cool. When it was still here in Utah we would take visitors to see it. I mean, it's so weird, you know? But then, it's pretty much a given that there's a serious history of mental illness in the art world."[11]

Natalie Carson expressed that the sculpture is, in part, a monument to people who "navigated the travails of life for such a long time." The artists seem to think these oral artifacts should be elevated to the status of keepsakes, monuments, or holy relics. "Teeth are one of our most distinctive body parts," said Carson. "Bodies are easily identified by dental records, and while dentures are not the same as natural teeth, I have always thought that we should keep teeth to remember our loved ones. They're far more personal than photographs. They're our best tool for breaking down food, for beginning the necessary transformation of food into usable energy. And if you think of the soul as light, as *energy*—and I do—teeth are practically the gateway to the soul."[12]

Carson's statement evokes the reliquaries of dead saints one finds in cathedrals and churches throughout Europe— tiny boxes filled with teeth or bones or the shreds of burial

---

[11] Ericka Roundy. Personal interview. November 7, 2014.

[12] Helena Robins. "Bite, Gnash, Nibble." *ARTnews*, May, 2013.

shrouds.[13] And Carson was indeed raised Catholic but attended mass (in English, not Latin) only until the age of thirteen, when she refused to attend ever again.

"Well, no, it wasn't okay with us," said Dominique Carson, Natalie's mother, of Natalie's lost faith. "But Nat was a headstrong girl. She locked herself in her bedroom and refused to answer my knocks. We were going to be late [for church], and it's not like I was going to break the door down, so we left her alone. That first time I grounded her, but even at thirteen she was able to articulate the reasons she did not believe in Catholicism, so she was allowed to stay home while the rest of the family attended mass, as long as she agreed to do something spiritual during that time."[14]

When asked what sorts of "spiritual" activities Carson participated in, her mother said that she was never entirely certain but that Natalie meditated sometimes and that the girl spent hours sitting on the porch watching birds feed. "Hummingbirds and red-winged blackbirds. She said nature was her church." It's rumored that in her later teenage years Carson created elaborate rituals, including the (burnt) sacrifice of mundane objects (pencil erasers,[15] shoelaces) and bodily cast-offs (fingernail clippings, eyebrow hairs) to various gods and spirits.

Carson's fixation on keepsakes and the material remains of loved ones may stem from a tragic backstory: the loss of her younger brother Edward when he was only nine years old (Carson was twelve; a year later she

---

[13] The writer once viewed the knuckle bone of Saint Catherine in a French cathedral, and in Bulgaria she saw a lock of hair nested in a tiny wooden box that purportedly came from the scalp of Saint John the Baptist. The writer was skeptical, however, of this second relic because the hair was honey-colored—a golden curl—and John, having been from the Middle East, was most certainly a dark-skinned man with dark hair.

[14] Dominique Carson. Telephone interview. November 12, 2014.

[15] Pencil erasers smell absolutely horrendous when burnt.

ceased attending mass). Edward died of leukemia, even after a bone marrow transplant (Natalie Carson was his donor), but Carson has consistently refused to discuss the loss of her young brother.

The genesis of *Denture House* occurred on Carson's porch during the summer of 2012, when Carson and Moulton were perusing employment ads on the local website *ksl.com*. The two were graduate students[16] and lacked stipends or employment during the summer months. They spent the month of May drinking whisky and gin and chalking stories on the sidewalk (their longest story spanned seventeen blocks: one sentence scrawled in all caps at each intersection and accompanied by taunts of "To be continued"), but by the end of the month they were desperate for money.[17]

It was Carson's half-birthday, and Moulton had baked a cake, sliced it in half, and frosted each half with pink and white buttercream. The platter was heavy, the halves slightly lopsided. The women drank gin and tonics with their cake and watched people bicycle past. Carson went into the house for fresh drinks, and when she returned, a small tissue-wrapped package rested on the porch rail. She unwrapped layer after layer of tissue, finally reaching the gift: a human molar on a gold chain.

"Wow!" she said, holding it up. The tooth swung back and forth, tick-tock. "Is it real? Is it yours?"

"I got it on Etsy years ago, but it seemed just right for you. Yeah, it's real."

---

[16] Carson in Cultural Anthropology; Moulton in Art History. Had they been more driven, they would probably have had internships or research projects during summer, as did most of their colleagues. Moulton admits she was depressed and drinking too much while Carson professes a lifetime of underachievement, lack of planning, and "general bafflement."

[17] Here, the writer takes "biopic" liberties, reconstructing the birth of *Denture House* based on conversations with the artists. Dialog is not verbatim.

Carson inspected the tooth. The roots were much whiter than the crown, which was distinctively yellow.[18] "It's huge!"

"It came with a tag that named and described its original owner and stuff, but I lost it. I think it belonged to an old man."

Carson put the tooth on. It rested in the lowest part of her V-neck.

"Sexy," she said. "I love it." She raised her glass, took a gulp, then leaned over and forcefully kissed her friend's forehead.

Salt Lake City is a banking town, and south of the city is one of the world's craft industry hubs,[19] but the employment ads were sparse. The Elizabeth Cutler Haven House was offering fifteen dollars per hour for aides (*will train*), a respectable hourly wage in their small city.

"I could do that," said Moulton. "I like old people. They've got stories."

Carson nodded. "But you might have to change diapers and wipe asses. And dementia is godawful depressing."

"I don't think it would bother me. It might even be fun. It taps the imagination, makes for good stories."

Carson made air quotes: "Even dementia can be fun," she said. "You should get that on a tee shirt."

"No, really. What if you think of it like hallucinatory drugs?"

Carson laughed. "Okay, Lu. You should do it. Really. I'd love to be an elderly person in your care."

"Think of all the tooth necklaces one could make in a place like that. An endless supply of materials," said Moulton.

---

[18] The writer has seen this necklace, which the artists excluded from the sculpture because they did not know its owner and because Carson still enjoys wearing the necklace. It appears to be a wisdom tooth, though the artists, despite their intimate knowledge of teeth, were unable to confirm my observation.

[19] Scrapbooking and rubber stamps.

And so they combed their hair and buttoned their cuffs. They were hired on the spot. But how did they do it? How did they acquire the teeth? And didn't their charges notice that their dentures were missing? "Sometimes we just asked for them," said Moulton.[20] "The residents liked us. Okay, we may have taken advantage of their exhausted judgment sometimes, but mostly it was easy." She waved a hand as if parting a curtain, conjuring the scene. Her storytelling voice was slower and deeper. "The old lady leans back against her pillow. Sleep. Finally, sleep. She slips her dentures from her mouth—*slurrrp*—and drops them into the glass of fizzy water. She's off to dreamland, galloping with wild horses, shimmying up ships' ladders. From the hallway, I crack the door. I listen for her breathing, that soft, sandy rhythm. I slip in, fish the dentures from the glass with a pair of tongs, drop them in a ziplock, and leave behind a daisy or something. And voila! You've been visited by the tooth fairy, darling dear."

Before the writer viewed *Denture House* she expected something morbid, humorous, and creepy: seventy-two sets of dentures, seventy-two frozen grins. So many disembodied gnashers poised to tap dance, threatening a nip. And the sheer number of teeth did not disappoint. The slick pink gums: pale or peachy or ruddy, purple-edged and dark, rising like the wings of butterflies, lumpy and gleaming, glistening like chewing gum, the satin petals of poppies and roses. Rows of teeth, so perfectly imperfect. Replicated overbites and underbites. Sharp canines and gaps and yellowings. Whole sets and half sets, biting and yawning.

But the tower isn't the stuff of nightmares. And it's only funny for a minute. And then the pink caves, the gaps and arches and tunnels, the missing mouths, the missing faces, the missing bodies and lost voices invite

---

[20] Personal interview. December 1, 2014.

you closer. Enter these tiny ballrooms. Rest in these tents of childhood summers, this ripstop-filtered sunlight. Even bees doze in this sleepy light. The pollen settles. In this precarious hive of souls.

Denture House is included in MOMA's *Dust to Dust: Sculpture and the Afterlife*, September 15-February 3. It is part of the museum's permanent collection.

LHOMME LETRE.

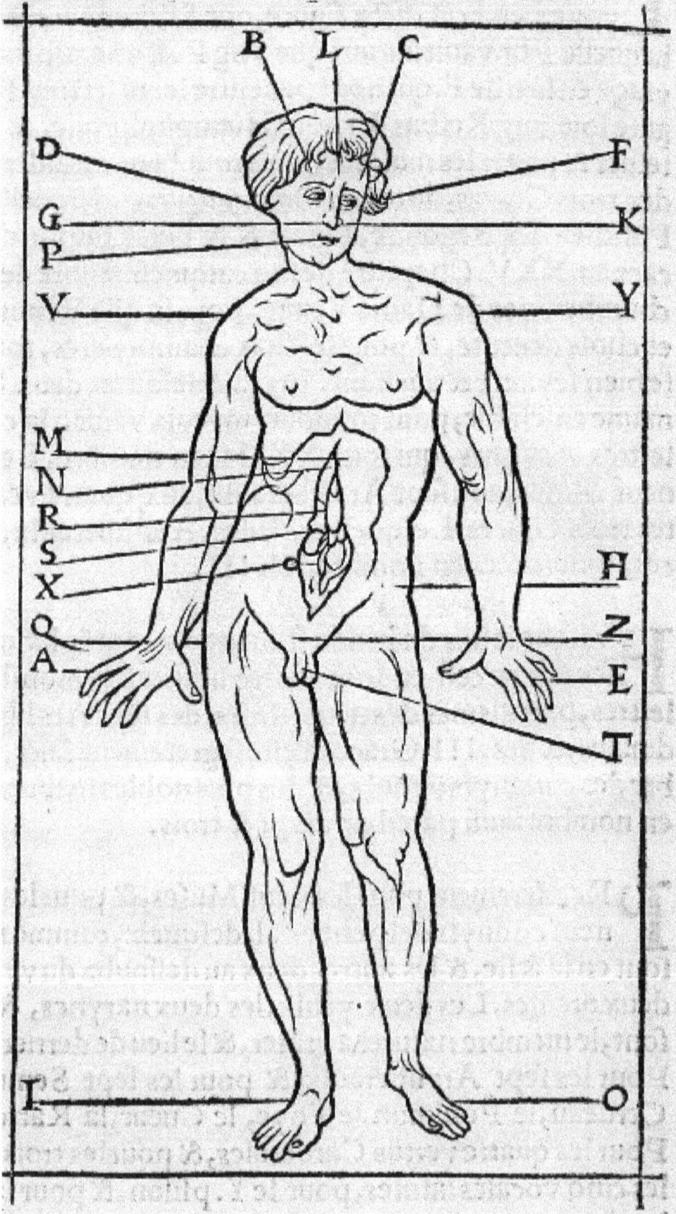

THE MUGGED BODY

(X) like a seashell. A conch, swallowed and lodged. Indigestible. The bruising appetite. A sound like the ocean roaring: listen. (X) is imagined. Where Quinn would have been cut if he had not given the mugger his wallet. If, instead, he had turned toward the man who was pressing a knife against his kidney. (X) is the blade remembered, swallowed and roaring between his diaphragm and his bladder.

(D) is his sweet ear, the half-deaf one, tucked beneath his wig (coarse, blond, synthetic, also indigestible).

(G) and (K) wheeze, sticky with the soot of winter. The skies of Quinn's town are always brown with copper tailings and desert sand, with salt and particles of disintegrated brine shrimp, car exhaust, mud, and wood smoke. Companions (G) and (K) whistled slightly as Quinn walked from the gym to his car, his keys jingling, swinging from (A). The parking lot was empty.

(I) is the ankle Quinn twisted when the mugger shoved him into the wall and ran off with his wallet. (I) was not broken but suffered a sprain and some bruising.

(O) is the bunion that has plagued Quinn since those nights—so many years ago now—when he used to squeeze his feet into such narrow shoes. Night after night, into slippers and stilettos. A tailor's bunion, it is called, because tailors sat cross-legged to sew, their pinky toes pressed for hours into the floor. Some call it a bunionette instead—a diminutive word, a diminutive thing. And Quinn babied his bunionette. He iced it on bad days. He named it Anabelle, an elaborate mouthful. The pain of (O) has been dwarfed by the new pain of (I).

(P) stayed quiet the whole time. (P) did not so much as whimper. Quinn's teeth bit (P) in fear. Quinn tasted blood and salt.

If (V) and (Y) were wings, Quinn would have flown instead of stumbling and spraining his ankle. Instead of digging his wallet out of his pocket (*such tight jeans, goddamn*) and handing it over. (*The right thing to do,* said the cops. *You'd have gotten yourself gutted or killed if you fought him. Not worth it to play the tough guy. Never worth it.*) But (V) and (Y) are only tattooed with mistakes. On (V): Matisse's *Blue Nude*, not even finished, half filled with blue ink, half hollow. The outline black. On (Y): Gerhard Richter's *Kerze*, the painting of the candle that also graces the cover of Sonic Youth's *Daydream Nation*. A white taper, the flame glowing on a background of divided gray rectangles (dark corner/light corner/tabletop). The tattoo is horribly faded. Quinn regrets the failed dimensionality of both tattoos. Representations of representations. Flatness that undulates with his skin. *Next time,* Quinn says, *an anchor. Next time, a mermaid.*

(B) is the eyebrow Quinn arches when skeptical or joking.

(C) is the eyebrow he cannot control.

(L) is his furrow of worry or guilt. A deep crease.

(E) is the finger that pointed at an innocent man in the lineup. It had been dark, after all, and panic distorts memory. Certainly, it had been a man. A man a little taller than Quinn. A man with hot breath and a voice that was almost a whisper. Yes, it had most certainly been a man. A man who smelled of onions. But the lineup was too far away for Quinn to smell the men, and they stood behind glass. Anyway, it had been hours since the man had pressed the knife against Quinn's ribs and prodded at his kidney. The mugger may have brushed his teeth since then. Quinn pointed at the most oniony-looking man of the bunch. The one whose skin was nearly translucent and webbed with tender blue. The one who looked the most heartless.

Anatomy texts label (H) the *iliacus*, but David, Quinn's lover, calls (H) "cupid's arrow." It is one of David's favorite body parts. He says the arrow is definitively male. *Oh, the superior musculature of a man's hips,* says David, tracing Quinn's arrow with his finger. They are home, finally. The mugging over. The lineup over. The pointing over. *Such perfect geometry,* David murmurs. His finger makes its way along the arrow to Quinn's left testicle (T), which is a smidgen smaller than his right one (unlabeled). David rolls (T) between his thumb and forefinger—a decidedly unsexy move. It feels vaguely medical to Quinn, but then David replaces his mechanical fingers with his soft mouth, and Quinn leans back against the pillows.

Later, in the dark, (F) hears David's chortling snore, hears hail strike the window. (F) hears the cat crying (she is trapped in the cabinet with the toaster and the blender—she is hungry). (F) hears the mugger's raspy voice, over and over: *Quiet now, mister. Real slow now. I want you to reach your hand in your pocket and take out your wallet. Slow now. Quiet now.* (F) hears the sandpaper voice. The lips that opened for the voice had been so close to (F). So close. The oniony breath had entered (F). And the words—*Slow. Quiet*—set (F)'s little bones vibrating. (Because [F] is full of little bones and whorls and tiny hairs that keep Quinn upright.) (F)'s little hairs trembled. Quinn tries to sleep, but over and over that fine-grit voice, that not-quite-a-whisper. But in the morning (F) hears traffic and bird songs. Bird songs in midwinter. Birds singing in all those black, leafless branches, those angry naked branches. So full of birds. (F) hears wings flap and scatter. (F) listens.

THE OTHER MATTER

In the thirteenth year since Odysseus's disappearance, when Tellie had reached junior high and was busy with sports and his budding social life, Odysseus's wife, Penelope, a renowned textile artist, called a press conference. She announced that she would begin a long project to mark the time since her husband's disappearance. She would weave a shroud in which to wrap her father-in-law's body when he died. The completion of the burial shroud would mark that it was time for Penny to accept that Odysseus was either dead or irrevocably lost, and at that time, she would go ahead and marry one of the many suitors who visited her house each day (for if Odysseus was dead, Penelope was a very wealthy woman—she would inherit the city house, the farm, everything). Thus, the completion of the shroud would impose closure. However, the project would take some time because she would weave it from superfine silk. It would be the most beautiful piece she had woven to date.

Everyone could see that Laertes was growing old, and grief over his missing son, and now the recent death of his wife, made the aging process especially violent, certainly more transformative than it would have been for a happier man. In the flurry of articles and opinion pieces that followed Penny's announcement, one columnist questioned whether Old Man Laertes would be able to accept the loss of his son on Penny's timeline. Or did Penny simply recognize that Laertes would never accept his son's death, could never move on? Thus, the columnist proposed, when Penny completed the weaving, Laertes would die. More than the shroud, Laertes's death would provide the closure they all lacked surrounding Odysseus's disappearance. Laertes's body would serve as a surrogate for the missing body of his son. Penny would wrap Laertes in the cloth, and in burying him, she would release both men into death and release the rest of Ithaca back into life. The world would resume turning. The time of waiting would come to an end.

After the press conference, Laertes found that he could not stay at the city house any longer. In the city house, he imagined a hundred different ways his son may have died, and he was consumed with thoughts of his own impending death, envisioning his body emaciated and then that suffocating shroud wrapped tightly around him, earth heaped over him. And so Laertes left the house where Penny and Tellie lived, and he moved out to the farm, twenty miles from the town center.

In his first year there, he built a wooden fence around the land and increased production, growing enough to feed himself and the handful of seasonal workers. In subsequent years, with the help of his workers, he grew enough to sell fruit at the local market each week: pears, apples, figs, and grapes, and in the nineteenth summer since Odysseus's disappearance, Laertes began fermenting wine, which they drank at communal dinners on the farm. He had given a barrel of it to Penny, and she declared that it was good enough for guests, so Laertes planned to triple his wine production in the fall. He might even make some of that sparkling wine with the green grapes. Word was that it was very popular these days, though frankly, Laertes found that it gave him a headache.

On the farm, Laertes had released his old, luxurious life day by day. He did not miss extravagant meals in the city, parties with wine and gin, afternoons at the golf club, custom shoes and silks, gossip and poker games, clouds of cigar smoke, or the press conferences. He had learned so many new things. Teresa, the woman he had hired to cook meals for him and his workers, taught him how to darn and patch his clothes, for one of his workers, Luis, had told Laertes about the river that ran along the northern edge of his hometown, a village near Nogales, Mexico, and how it ran pink or blue or green depending on the color of the dye the textile factory was using that day. The garments they made from those textiles were meant to last only a season before they fell apart or were considered unfashionable. The apparel factories weren't the only problem for the river, Luis said, not at all, but whether it was from textile dyes, agricultural byproducts, waste from plastics and electronics, or untreated sewage, the townspeople had grown sicker over the years. People died of cancer or suffered from mysterious, undiagnosed ailments, especially rashes and respiratory conditions. Laertes decided if he did not know a shirt's path from plant to tailor, he would not buy it. And his clothes were fine anyway, he said, shrugging. Why not wear them until they fell from his body like the meat from a pit-smoked hog? The next clothing he would wear, he said, would be the funerary shroud.

In winter, Laertes lived in a one-room shack. Inside, there was a pellet stove, a cot, and a corduroy armchair where Laertes sat to watch the dust drift in the sun that fell through the dirty windows. The particles made the light tangible, and if light could become material, so might the human spirit, which meant he might some-day encounter the soul of his lost son and recognize him. Odysseus's spirit would be as golden as a winter sunbeam.

Back when Odysseus was a boy, Laertes had brought him to the farm sometimes. It was just a small orchard back then, but Laertes had taught Odysseus the name of each apple and pear varietal, and they had tried them all. Odysseus was a messy eater, and the juice would run between his fingers and along his arms to his elbows. Messy eating, Laertes always said, was a sign that a man knew how to enjoy life. *Pleasure over order*, Laertes said. But he also reminded the boy that there was more to life than pleasure.

Laertes himself was a dainty eater. Even as the years passed and grief tattered him, he ate meticulously. It was a compulsion he could not overcome. For Laertes, eating neatly was part of the pleasure, a way of honoring his food and his dining companions. He even ate his apples with a knife, being constitutionally unable to bite into the flesh directly. His wife, dead now for seven years, had always called him her *dear raccoon* because raccoons are the neatest of the animals, always taking time to wash their food and their paws in streams or puddles, never letting scraps linger on their whiskers or lips.

During the warmer months, Laertes slept in a hammock strung between two apple trees. He loved spring best because the blossoms were his deepest pleasure. Who doesn't love a blizzard of pale pink petals, the softness of spring air in one's lungs after the frost has finally gone? Each morning, Laertes lay in his hammock and looked up through the matrix of branches to the blue sky.

Laertes and his workers tended tirelessly to the fruit trees, espaliering the limbs of the pears along the fence so they looked like elaborate menorahs. From the soil, they coaxed rows of blue onions and chives and scrubby rosemary, clusters of mint and oregano, tomatoes and carrots and beets. Laertes found that he loved tending to growing things and that when he was in his garden or among the trees, his grief settled some, and he did not worry so much about his own impending death. He was more at ease with other people. He could spend hours with his workers in silence and it never felt awkward because they were all bent to their tasks. At the end of the day, they all ate dinner together in the courtyard, where there was an outdoor kitchen between their shacks and hammocks. Teresa spread the food out on a long board set atop sawhorses, and everyone filled their bowls and feasted. Laertes loved these dinners—how hungry he was after the long day of work! And the setting sun made the world glow.

On one such evening, lingering over a glass of wine, catching distant strains of a harmonica being played in the orchard, Laertes had the thought that if his son had not gone to Troy and disappeared, then he, Laertes, might never have known this part of life—the apple blossoms and the company of the men with whom he worked—and while Laertes wouldn't go as far as to say he was *grateful* to have lost his son, he was at least glad to know this sweetness that suddenly made his eyes brim over with joy.

Over time, Laertes learned where each of his workers had come from, which was mostly Mexico, though some were from Honduras or El Salvador. While he loved the farm, he knew that it was not home to his workers, that they worked in order to live and to take care of their families, who were elsewhere. Ignacio, who had soft, brown curls that he always tucked into his hat, had three children and a wife back in Tegucigalpa, and he sent almost all of his pay to them. Unlike Luis, who had told Laertes about the pollution in Nogales, Ignacio did not want to bring his family to the U.S. but instead hoped to earn enough money that he could return home and run his mother's pupuseria without worry, and that his children could get the education they wanted, whether that meant college or culinary school or even business school. He hoped one of them might even franchise the pupuseria. For Ignacio, saving money meant being able to return and remain in his hometown, to keep his roots intact, to give his children a home to which they could return.

Alejandro had left his Salvadoran village with his thirteen-year-old son because a local gang had been harassing and threatening the boy, who would, it seemed, eventually have to join a gang or die. Alejandro himself was powerless against them. He and his son had applied for asylum, but their case had been pending for a year now.

Laertes knew that Mitchell's favorite place in the whole world was Carwash Cenote, a natural sinkhole somewhere near Tulum where he had snorkeled when he was a boy, a place where lily pads waved gently and one could drift for hours in the bright blue water and then sit on shore eating lotus blossoms by the handful. ("What do you mean 'lotus blossoms'?" Laertes asked, but Mitchell was unable to translate any other way. "It is an edible flower," Mitchell said. "They make you dreamy.")

All of Laertes's workers knew about Odysseus, too. When Laertes's eyes welled with tears because he was thinking of his son, they hugged him or sat up late with him or began playing a new song on the guitar to lift the mood. Some of them knew what it was like to wait for a lost loved one, the way you sometimes even wished for news of the loved one's death or the discovery of their remains because at least this news put an end to the waiting and wondering, the stasis of grief that stretched across years.

Luis told Laertes about his brother one morning while they were installing a new irrigation hose. It had been three years ago, Luis said, before he had gotten the H1-Visa, and he and his brother had walked to the U.S. Their group had been walking quietly on a starry, cold night, somewhere in Arizona, excited that they were nearing the end of their time in the wilderness. Soon they would have fresh water and beds and showers. They could call their families. But then they ran into a Border Patrol Jeep. Searchlights and gunfire scattered the group, sending everyone running, and in the morning, when Luis uncurled from his hiding place among an outcropping of rocks, a few of the others also emerged from their hiding places and gathered again under the morning sky, but his brother was not among them. Luis found his way to a town, where he waited, hoping his brother would turn up, either in custody or on his own two feet. Luis called home every other day to see if his brother had made it back to Nogales, but his brother never arrived on either side of the border. There was no word. Luis wondered if one day a rancher or immigration officer or hiker might find his brother's bones, and if so, how would they know that it was him? So, yes, Luis knew what it meant to wait, to wonder, to grieve for someone who was neither dead nor alive.

That August, the twentieth since Odysseus's disappearance, Laertes turned seventy-three. Penny invited him into town to celebrate, but he said Teresa would make fruit pie and fresh ice cream, and he'd have a quiet celebration at the farm as he had for his last five birthdays. He invited Penny and Tellie to join him, but on the night of his birthday, only Tellie showed up. Tellie reported that his mother's gallerist had arrived from New York that afternoon, unannounced and anxious about how long it had been since Penny had completed any new work. Penny sent her regrets, but Tellie said that Laertes should be glad she had not chosen to bring the gallerist out to the farm. The man would probably be studying Laertes for signs of impending death because of the stupid shroud.

Tellie extended his hand, and in his palm rested a pair of golden cufflinks. "My mom sent these for you," he said. "Happy birthday, Grandpa."

Laertes could not imagine an occasion when cufflinks would make sense in his life, but he laughed and affixed the cufflinks to his tattered sleeves.

Tellie, nearly twenty-two now, had grown into a willowy young man who spent most of his time reading novels and almost always wore a huge pair of headphones nestled snugly over his ears. The headphones were around his neck now, a tinny beat spilling from them.

"Turn those things off and come have some dinner," Laertes said.

After dinner, when Teresa was scooping ice cream onto slices of pie, and Tellie had drifted to "listen to some tunes" in the orchard, Ignacio sat down next to Laertes and handed him a small flat box tied with a striped ribbon. Laertes opened it to find a pair of soft leather work gloves. The leather was supple and golden brown, punctuated with the distinctive triple follicles of peccary. It was a remarkable pair of gloves.

Ignacio spoke solemnly. "I did not personally know the animal from which these gloves came," he said, for he knew Laertes's rule about new clothing. "It was a wild animal in Peru, a boar that wandered free, untamed by humans, and it was hunted down in the forest, but it was my wife who tanned and stretched the leather, and she cut and sewed the gloves. I know that you work hard, and that you must protect your hands from the brambles. I hope you will agree that your hard work will honor the animal from which this skin was taken."

Laertes took the gloves from the box and pressed them to his cheek to feel their smoothness, and then pulled them on, one finger at a time, and wiggled his fingers gleefully. He pulled Ignacio in for a hug. "I will honor the animal and your wife and you, who have given me this gift," he said.

Laertes loved those gloves. When he wore them, he sometimes thought of the animal whose skin they were made from, a beast that had wandered in the mountains so far away. He began to think of the animal as a brother to Odysseus, who also wandered wild now, whether it was in earthly mountains or in the unknown valleys of the underworld.

Laertes was wearing the gloves on the day that Odysseus returned. Odysseus had gone first to the city house, his home, where he had been reunited with Penny. (She had abandoned the burial shroud, leaving it hanging limp on the loom. It would never be completed, but her gallerist would eventually sell it as a conceptual piece representing interruption and delay.) Laertes, however, had not yet heard the news of his son's return. He did not have a television or computer on the farm, and his only phone was a landline. Odysseus had not called to announce himself.

Odysseus stood at the gate and watched his father pat soil around the base of a vine. He noted that his father's clothing was worn and filthy, patched with visible seams, that Laertes looked like a beggar. Laertes's beard was tangled and stained yellow around the mouth. Twenty years ago, when Odysseus had left for the war, his father had been a strong man with a straight back and broad shoulders, no hint of white in his hair or beard, but now he looked old and sad and broken. Laertes smoothed his gloved hands over the dirt with tenderness that seemed extreme, as if the plant were a child or perhaps even a lover.

Penny had reported that Laertes had gotten "eccentric," that it had been over three years since he had set foot in the house, and possibly as long since he had been to town at all. She worried that the old man was sliding into dementia, though she admitted that stubbornness or reclusiveness did not necessarily indicate that Laertes was losing his mind. Thank the gods, Odysseus thought, that Laertes had contained himself out here and was not wandering through the city streets collecting cans or making a fool of himself and the family in front of the media back at the house. He cringed to think of the news headlines, the photos they'd run: *Hero Returns to Find His Father at Death's Door; Father of Long-Lost Odysseus Now a Hermit.* Odysseus would do his best to protect his father from scorn or ridicule now that he was back. He, Odysseus, would take control of the finances, get things back on track, get his father the medical care he surely needed. He'd get Laertes to move back into the city house, where he could bathe regularly and they could keep an eye on him.

At least this reunion would be private. Odysseus sighed at the weight of it all, the hullaballoo his arrival was sure to cause. In a way, he wished he could slip back into his life quietly, skip the drama, the questions, the press conferences, the whole media circus, the legal paperwork that was surely in his future as he sorted through his holdings. But on the other hand, he had a million stories to tell, and he wanted to tell them! He had seen monsters. He had tricked a cyclops. He had been wooed by a sexy goddess. He wasn't some average middle-aged golf pro like some of the men he'd grown up with. He wasn't measuring his life out with coffee spoons or charitable donations. He was an adventurer, and he wanted his rightful adventurer's welcome. He wanted nights of feasting and storytelling—like last night, which he had spent in bed with his wife, telling stories between the tussles. Now that he was back, he had to admit he had really missed Penny.

But would his father even recognize him? Laertes would be surprised, certainly. Quite possibly over-whelmed. Odysseus was middle-aged now, stouter and ruddier than he had been when he left. He had spent a lot of time in the sun, after all, and it had been years since he and his men had run out of sunscreen. What's more, his father's vision was clouded by cataracts. Laertes looked frail. What if the surprise of Odysseus's return caused Laertes to have a heart attack or a stroke? What if he wept? Odysseus hated weeping. It embarrassed him. It would be best, Odysseus decided, to feel out the situation anonymously. He'd pretend to be someone else, get the lay of the land, find out just how far gone his father was. He stepped into the garden.

"Old man," Odysseus said. Laertes looked up and studied him with cloudy eyes. "Whose farm is this? Who is it that makes you work so hard? An old man like you should be resting." Laertes squinted at him and he stepped closer. Laertes still said nothing. "Is this Ithaca, old man? A fellow I met back there on the road told me that it was, but I thought Ithaca would be a grander place. A town at least. I thought it was a city."

"This is it," Laertes said. "The outskirts of it anyway. The city itself is a few miles down the road. You can see the skyline there." He gestured to the west although he could no longer see the distant buildings himself.

"I was hoping to find a friend here," Odysseus said. "A man I met once years ago, a traveler who told me that Ithaca was his home. He said that it was full of the most beautiful women and that there were craftspeople who carved intricate furniture from the bases of old trees, that there were plentiful vineyards and antique shops. He said that it was a progressive place, with lots of jobs in wind and solar. He waxed on about the wide bike trails and a city park with free music in the summer. But this looks more or less like an average town to me. A little beaten down. A little rusty. The road is full of potholes!"

"This man you met," Laertes said, ignoring the details Odysseus had listed. "Who was he? How did you meet him? And where?"

"I met him in Crete," Odysseus said. "My hometown. We really hit it off, me and this Odysseus. He stayed with me for a few weeks, and when he left, I loaded him up with gifts—with golden cups and handwoven rugs he said his wife would love. He took grafts from our fruit trees for his father."

Laertes's eyes filled with tears that threatened to spill down his cheeks. Perhaps he was being cruel, Odysseus thought for the first time, but he could not stop himself. "You know him? This Odysseus?"

Laertes tried to speak, but finally he just shook his head in silence. He leaned into the dirt on his hands and knees.

"Old man!" Odysseus bellowed. He clapped Laertes on the shoulder. "It's me! It's *me*! *I* am Odysseus! By gods, I thought you'd know me, your own son! Your boy!"

Laertes looked up and squinted at him again. He wiped the tears from his eyes with the backs of his gloves. He stood and leaned close to Odysseus, closer, until Odysseus could feel his father's breath in his face, and smell it, too—many years without a dentist.

"Is it you?" Laertes whispered. "Odysseus? Is it you?"

"Look!" Odysseus said, and scrunched his pants up to his knee. "This scar! You know it! I got it hunting wild pigs when I was fifteen!"

Laertes took off his gloves and touched the pale half-moon scar with two fingers as if he were reading braille. Odysseus was surprised to see that his father's hands were clean and manicured, though his fingertips were calloused.

"That could have been a disaster," Laertes whispered. "You could have lost your leg."

"You know me, then? What else?" He looked around. "These trees!" He pulled Laertes toward the edge of the orchard and pointed. "Cortland," he said. "And over there are the Pink Ladies. And down at the other end are the Romes. And the pear trees! They were not espaliered like that when I was young! You taught me their names, their leaves, the flavors of their fruits. You walked me up and down the rows until I knew them all."

They stood for a minute, eye to eye, and it seemed to Odysseus that his father grew taller and straighter, as if he, Odysseus, were the sun, or maybe the rain, and Laertes was a thirsty plant. They embraced, and then Laertes did as Odysseus had feared and wept loudly onto his shoulder. "My boy!" he sobbed. "My son! You're here! You're alive!"

When they stepped apart, Laertes gave Odysseus another long look, admiring his size, the proud tilt of his head. Odysseus was not a boy any longer but a man with weathered skin and some extra heft. Laertes noted a new scar above Odysseus's eyebrow, the gray at his temples. Laertes thought, not for the first time, that Tellie was now almost the age Odysseus had been when he left for the war, and yet Tellie seemed impossibly young. He still barely needed to shave and went by his childhood nickname, which was hardly fit for an adult man, but then his parents had saddled him with such an elaborate name. Perhaps he could go by Machus, which had sharper, more angular sounds. Laertes wondered if Odysseus had seen Tellie yet, but he would save that conversation for later.

"Are you hungry?" Laertes asked. "We eat together every evening out here, but your arrival warrants an early quitting time, I'd say. A real feast is in order!"

Odysseus said that he had already sent his men ahead to find the cook, to slaughter a pig or a goat. "Forgive the presumption," Odysseus said with a nod.

"Of course!" Laertes did not tell Odysseus that he was vegetarian now, that many of the men who worked for him were also vegetarian. It was a special occasion, after all, and people associated meat with celebration. Laertes might even eat a little pork himself, he thought, but then he pictured his goats, his pigs, the animals he sometimes conversed with as if they could understand him. He had a number of animals butchered each fall and sold the meat, but he had his workers do the dirty work. *Have I not earned this complacency?* he joked, but it was true that he did not like to look closely at pain of any kind.

Laertes and Odysseus walked between the grape vines to the other end of the garden, a distance of nearly half a mile, and turned to walk along the fence where the workers' shacks stood.

"So much has changed," Odysseus said. He gestured to the shacks. "These little hovels. I don't remember them. They're well-kept, if modest. And the plants— it's an impressive plot, Old Man. Your green thumb has flourished while I've been away. The plants seem in better health than you, if you'll forgive my saying so."

Laertes smiled. "I take that as a compliment."

They had arrived at the kitchen where Teresa was presiding over the workers, preparing a meal. Luis was chopping onions and tomatoes for salsa while Ignacio was standing over the grill with a set of metal tongs. Everyone paused as Odysseus and Laertes approached. It was silent until Luis stepped forward and shook Odysseus's hand.

"Welcome home," he said. "We are so honored to be here with you on this day. Your father has waited for this moment for so many years, though perhaps none of us truly believed it would come."

"Thank you," Odysseus said. "I'm glad to be home." Luis held Odysseus's hand in both of his and bowed a little. Odysseus blushed, so Luis released him. Smiling broadly, he returned to his cutting board.

Laertes and Odysseus sat in wooden Adirondack chairs with their feet propped on the cinder block fire ring. The air was spiced with the smells of roasting meat that made even the vegetarians' mouths water. People began to eat, and then some of the workers got out musical instruments, and Teresa brought Laertes his guitar, and soon there was music and singing, the occasional impromptu jig between plates heaped with roasted veggies and meats, endless cups of wine. Even Odysseus, who was not musically inclined, sang in a quavering voice about a long-lost sailor, and everyone clapped.

The feasting and dancing went on until dusk, when it was time to wash up and get to bed, for there was work to do the next day. The workers drifted off into the night, but Odysseus and Laertes sat up longer, sipping wine, their feet propped again on the stones around the dying fire. There were so many stories to tell, and Odysseus told a few of them—the beach where his men had gotten stoned by eating flowers, the stupid cyclops he had outwitted. He began telling Laertes about a goddess who had detained him, seducing him magically for many years, but he kept forgetting parts of the story and backing up to revise things until Laertes assured his son that they had time, that there was no need to tell everything tonight, though of course he wondered where his son had been these twenty years. Mostly, Laertes assured Odysseus, he was just glad Odysseus was back.

And so they were sitting in silence when Luis returned and sat down on a stump beside Laertes and began to speak, quietly, as if worried about waking the others.

"Laertes, sir, I spoke with my wife this evening."

Laertes nodded.

"She tells me that my sister-in-law has been detained at the border with her two-year-old daughter and that they have taken her daughter from her. They told her it was only for the night, for medical checks, but now they say they will send my sister-in-law back to Mexico. They'll keep the girl until her mother completes the appropriate paperwork. She has not seen her daughter in five days."

Laertes sat up in his chair. "What do you mean? They took a two-year-old from her mother? Who is caring for the girl? Where is your sister-in-law now?"

"I don't know exactly," Luis said. "Not everything is clear. What I know is that my sister-in-law is in detention with many others, and they allowed her to call my wife once. And her daughter is not with her. She does not know where her daughter is or who is caring for her."

"She's in Arizona?" Laertes asked.

"Texas."

"Texas," Laertes repeated. He stood up and began to pace. "Texas," he said again. "What do you need, Luis? How can I help?"

"I think I must go to Texas." Luis, too, stood up, but he did not pace. He stared into the fire, his face glowing with its light, expressionless.

"Yes," Laertes said. He nodded emphatically. "You should go. Tomorrow?"

Luis nodded.

"How will you get there?"

"The bus."

"It will take days," Laertes said.

Odysseus watched the two men from his chair, his feet still propped on the fire ring, eyes moving back and forth between his father and Luis. Neither of them looked at him.

"If you don't get there until next week, your sister-in-law may be back in Mexico already," Laertes said.

"I know," said Luis. His arms hung limply at his sides.

"And it's too long for her to be away from her daughter."

"I know."

"You should fly. I'll buy you a ticket," Laertes said. "First thing in the morning, we'll go to the airport." He turned to Odysseus. "Son," he said, "can you arrange a car for us?"

Odysseus looked startled. He uncrossed his feet and sat up, set his feet on the ground, gave a small cough. "I don't have a car," he said.

"From town, of course," Laertes said. "Have Penny send someone. I don't drive anymore. Or you could just arrange a cab."

Odysseus pursed his lips as if preparing to speak, but he said nothing for a long time. He shook his head a little, side to side, but it was unclear to Laertes if this meant he was thinking or if he was saying no, he would not arrange the car.

"Never mind," Laertes said, finally. "I'll have Teresa call a cab in the morning." He turned from Odysseus and put his hand on Luis's shoulder. "I wish that I could say everything will be fine," he said.

Luis nodded gravely. "I know."

"You should sleep. You should try to sleep." Laertes hugged him and they stood that way for a minute, until Luis stepped away from him.

"Thank you."

"We will do what we can," he said. "You will do what you can." He took Luis's hand and squeezed it, and Luis nodded. "It's a terrible thing that's happening."

Luis nodded again and turned to walk back to his lodging, for he could not talk about his worries. He did not want to name them aloud.

Laertes turned to Odysseus. "I'm going to bed," he said. "I'll show you where you can sleep." Odysseus stood and followed his father.

For hours, Laertes lay awake in his hammock. Through the branches, he could make out the blurry stars, but they brought no peace. He squinted to bring them into focus but they remained smeary and scrambled. He had only asked Odysseus to arrange a car, nothing more, and yet Odysseus would not do it. Laertes turned onto his shoulder, though the hammock was not comfortable that way. He got up. Where had Odysseus been all these years? What had he seen? Perhaps he had been imprisoned somewhere? But if that were the case, would he not have more compassion for a woman imprisoned, a child imprisoned, a child alone? Laertes shook his head.

Laertes knew that Luis loved Mexico. That he missed his village and his family, but his home had been destroyed. There was no living to be made there any longer. There was death in the water and in the drug traffickers in the nearby towns and in the gangs. The wages were so low that Luis could not feed his family. Laertes did not know what exactly had forced Luis's sister-in-law to undertake a journey that put her and her child in harm's way, but he knew that no one would choose to walk through the desert like that unless they truly felt it was their best option.

Eventually, Laertes found that he had slept, for he awoke as the sun was rising. He was brewing coffee in the outdoor kitchen when Odysseus stepped out of the shack where he had slept, stretching and scratching and groaning, stripped down to a T-shirt and a threadbare pair of sweatpants. His feet were bare.

Laertes's gloves were on the countertop, and Odysseus picked them up and began to inspect them, running his fingers over the neat stitches, examining the patterns of the follicles, rumpling them up and unfolding them again to feel how soft they were, how pliable.

"Where'd you get these?" he asked. "They're exquisite."

"They were a gift," Laertes said. He reached for them, but Odysseus stepped back and put one of them on, flexed his hand, stretched the leather, pulling it taut.

"Peccary, hmm?" Odysseus pulled the other glove on and raised his hands out in front of him, stretching his ten fingers wide.

"Yes," said Laertes. "I see you know your leather." He poured hot water over the coffee grounds and inhaled the first smell of the beans.

Odysseus ran his gloved hands over his own face, feeling the rough texture of his stubbled jaw with the smooth skin of the gloves. "These men you employ," he said. "Where do you find them? Do they have visas?"

Laertes watched the water level lowering as it drained through the coffee, avoiding Odysseus's eyes. "Is that your concern?" he asked.

Odysseus began rubbing one hand along his arm like a cat grooming itself. "Well," he said, "this farm belongs to me. The house, too. All of it. The kegs of wine. The stores of food. Now that I'm back, I'll be overseeing things. I need to learn the ins and outs of my investments, and this farm is one of my investments. So yes, my concern."

"On paper," Laertes said, turning to him now. "It belongs to you on paper."

"Like I said, it belongs to me." He stopped rubbing the gloves along his arms and stood with his hands clasped together in front of him.

"Technically. As a business matter."

"What other matter is there?" Odysseus said. "I don't want to employ illegals."

Laertes studied him. The sun was in Odysseus's eyes now, but he did not move to avoid it, and the brightness showed the creases and age spots, the yellowed whites of his eyes. When Odysseus was gone, Laertes had imagined him as a lost animal, as a prisoner, as a ghost caught between life and death, but here he was, unlost and whole, sunburned and barefoot. It seemed now that Odysseus had wandered by choice, a leisurely vagabond, while at home his family waited, his city waited. Perhaps it was Laertes's fault for encouraging Odysseus to privilege pleasure when he was young. Nothing else could explain this lack of compassion, this talk of business, of money and ownership, even as peoples' lives were at stake, even as babies were taken from their parents' arms.

"The gloves," Laertes said. "They're special to me." He reached for them again, and Odysseus stepped back, but Laertes persisted. "They were a gift from Ignacio." The sun was at Laertes's back now, and his shadow darkened Odysseus's face. Luis would be up soon, ready to go to the airport, but for the moment it seemed that even the birds were silent, watching them from the trees around the courtyard, and the sun was suspended in its progress into the sky. "He has become like family to me these last few summers. So has Luis, and all of the workers. So that is the other matter. Or it is the only matter."

Laertes took Odysseus's hand and stripped the glove from it, finger by finger.

69218

THE COURSE TO THE HORIZON

We were fast men and the media loved us, John Cobb and me, George E.T. Eyston, friendly rivals and fellow Brits, racing across the American salt. At dawn, we gathered near the silver tent and took turns with the binoculars, inspecting the mountains that looked blue, though we knew they were brown and would show it when the sun was high. Everything was illusion at the Salt Flats: what looked like snow was salt. What looked like a scurrying lizard was the sleekest, fastest car in the world.

I watched from the tent as eight men carried the shell of Cobb's Railton Special. It looked like one of those Chinese dragons that dance in parades, a dragon from the future walking on a million human legs. The crew lowered the shell carefully over the frame, over Cobb himself, who was sitting in the seat, wearing his goggles and hood. My own car, the Thunderbolt, was heavier but more powerful. It looked like a blowfish with bulging eyes, an open mouth for air intake, and a fin to keep it steady. I loved the focus that driving demanded. My attention narrowed to the black line that marked my course to the horizon.

By midday the salt rose like fog in the wake of our tires. Cobb broke my land speed record that day, but I broke his the next. I hit 357.5 miles per hour, but a year later, in 1939, he took the record back, and then there was the war, and we all stopped racing for a time.

The next time Cobb broke the land speed record was in 1947, reaching 394.19 miles per hour. I was home in London then, a man with a wife and daughters, a man who had seen two wars, a tired man with a paunch. My Thunderbolt was on display in a New Zealand museum and then burned up in a warehouse fire, poor girl. But Cobb kept on. He broke my record and came home to London triumphant, married a woman named Glass, and turned his attention to the water, seeking new types of speed.

Every day for six weeks, he drove his speedboat on Loch Ness. I was there on the day the Queen came and shook his hand and wished him well, for we were friends, John Cobb and I. We were fast men, the fastest men, him a little faster than me. And I was there, too, on the day his boat reached 240 miles per hour. I was one of the crew, holding a clipboard, the competitions manager standing on shore beside Cobb's wife, who leaned down and kissed him before he fired up the engine. But the water was not as smooth as it appeared. The boat hit a wake and disintegrated in a puff. What looked like a water bug, what looked like an ice skate, what looked like a fishing lure or a lightning bolt or a flimsy piece of tin, was a man airborne, a man flying free, the body of the world's fastest man.

BENEVOLENCE

As a child, Eliza Farnham had an unremarkable head. Round and smooth, it had the proverbial soft spot at the crown where her skull had last knit itself together. But by her twenty-ninth year there had formed, at the apex of her cranium, a prominent bump. This bump was not particularly noticeable when one viewed Eliza directly, looking straight into her shadowy eyes, but when she turned to glance out at the bitter landscape or to reach for a book in some hidden corner of her office, it was suddenly evident, looking almost as if she had been recently clobbered and bruised.

According to phrenology, the bump was located in region thirteen of her skull, which housed the organ of benevolence, one in the conglomeration of organs that were her brain. Being her dominant organ, benevolence was swollen and pushed gently at the bone in which it was encased, resulting in the bump, outward evidence of Eliza's exaggerated goodwill.

In 1844, Eliza's husband was off exploring the wilds of California. Not to be outdone by his pioneering spirit, she determined to put her powerful organ to use in the new women's wing at a prison on the banks of the Hudson River. Thirty miles north of New York, and twenty years before Eliza's arrival, one hundred prisoners had quarried river rock and built the walls that would contain them. Through three frozen winters they worked, and when they finished it was Sing Sing: place of stone.

Eliza spent her first morning as prison matron sitting at a table in the corner of the mess hall, watching her charges and taking notes. In her notebook she drew the outlines of several skull shapes: simple busts, including profiles. Beneath each sketch she wrote the corresponding prisoner's name, which was provided for her by the Chaplain, John Luckey, who already detested her. Beneath the name she jotted speculations about the prisoners according to the shapes of their skulls. *Acquisitiveness?* she wrote beneath one sketch, and she turned to the Chaplain to inquire about this woman's crime. Larceny, he answered, and Eliza smiled in triumph.

As the prisoners settled for lunch, a straggler arrived, a guard close behind pressing a wooden club between her shoulder blades. The prisoner was young and strikingly attractive, with black hair and pale skin. Her eyes were steely; upon entering the room she cast them to the floor. She had a small head, perched delicately upon a slender neck and narrow shoulders. Her arms hung like plumb lines. Eliza stared, making no notes, sketching nothing, but when the Chaplain cleared his throat and stood to lead the prisoners in prayer, she rapidly sketched the girl's profile. The shape of her skull was apparent through her sleek hair, which was pulled into a tight plait that ran down her back like an external spine. In her sketch, Eliza captured—if not exaggerated—the prisoner's short forehead and the plateau, a divot even, on the front half of the top of her head. Behind that was a pronounced but dainty rise in the same place as Eliza's own most prominent bump. Eliza jotted *Pronounced benevolence* and beneath that *Deficiency of justice and self-esteem.* The prisoner's name, Eliza learned when the Chaplain finished his prayer, was Maria Giatti. Her crime was murder.

Yellow bile, black bile, blood, and phlegm: each courses in symphony through the veins. The trick to health lies in balancing the four. Here: a bilious woman, her temperament evident in her swarthy skin and close-set eyes, not to mention she refuses to peel potatoes; she spits in the dishwater. A spoonful of tartar emetic will thin her yellow bile. And this one's a melancholic— thin hair, high temples—she has a quick mind, but see how she slumps. She chatters her teeth. Practically brimming with black bile. Rub her skin with mustard, blister her arms, dose her with Calomel—a miracle in a teaspoon. The sanguine, face full and ruddy, paces her cell and sighs—too much blood rushing through her veins. Leeches should do the trick. And the phlegmatic is soft and round, with jowls and a bulbous nose. For this underwater mover, snuffling in her sleep—a handful of prickly ash steeped in tea will quicken her.

Eliza walked with certainty—quickly, head up. She made and held eye contact with everyone, even the prisoners when they would look at her. She never slipped quietly into a room but burst into it, flinging the door aside like a discarded petticoat. Certainty pervaded more than her movements. Over tea with the Chaplain, on her first day as matron, she confessed: she detested God and despised His Word. No one had ever sat beside her with a Bible spread across her lap, and that suited her just fine. She had no mother or father. She had been raised by an older brother and then by an aunt, whom she hated.

"No need to dwell on those particular illusions," she said. "I've made it this far in life on my own—from my aunt's musty old house to the Illinois prairie and back again. I intend to keep on ticking." Already, at twenty-nine, she had outlived two of her three sons. The one still alive, she said, was like her: tenacious and stringy.

"Like a piece of jerky," the Chaplain said, under his breath.

"I can reform these women," Eliza said. "But I suppose we'll go about things differently. For you, if I may presume, God is responsible for saving them. For me, salvation lies in understanding their brains."

By Eliza's system, the brain consisted of a mass of organs, each named for the trait it controlled—violence, for example, or amativeness. The organs were organized in a logical manner, with the baser, animalistic "propensities" clustered in the lower back half of the skull, and the noble "sentiments" nesting in the top front. A criminal was born with a skewed hierarchy of organs—propensities were overdeveloped and sentiments withered. With the proper influence, order could be restored—sentiments plumped and propensities shriveled. Eliza was at Sing Sing to be the proper influence.

The Chaplain dropped a lump of sugar into his tea, which splashed onto the tablecloth. He was a small man, not at all like Eliza's husband. Smaller, even, than Eliza, and sitting knee to knee with her, he looked frail. He pushed his hair across his forehead. It was thin, pale hair, shaggy around the ears, which poked through. His jaw, though, was square, and his mouth vividly pink. His eyes were blue. He stirred his tea, sloshing it into his saucer.

"You're right," he said. "Our methods differ." He pressed his lips together and folded his napkin. Then he unfolded it.

Eliza grew accustomed to the heavy scrape of metal on metal, the squall of fifty locks opening simultaneously. Fifty doors sliding on their tracks. Fifty prisoners murmuring, standing, blinking in the gray light that seeped from the corridor into their cells. Her charges had been found guilty of an array of crimes: petit and grand larceny, villainy, arson, assault and battery, murder. As a whole, they were of a sanguine nature, flushed and confident and disconcertingly optimistic. Some of the women would spend the rest of their lives within those cold walls, but they had shelter, they had food. Had they also comprehension of their situation? Eliza concluded that some did and that others were incapable of comprehension. These women, Eliza thought, would have cheerfully endured the fate of Sisyphus. This inability to comprehend the misery of their lives was sometimes evidenced by a flatness above the eyebrows, beneath which lived the organ of time.

That ticking metronome: a fiddle saws and the dancers step together, twirl. The sun casts her shadows: long, short, long. Bare trees bud and unfurl. First tender, then tough, their leaves turn yellow. They come loose. They are lost under snow.

A baby grabs her mother's hair, her mother's breast, a cookie resting on a plate. She learns the alphabet and that she is a girl. She wants new shoes, a slice of pie, a train ride, a man's touch. These are granted. The man wipes his nose with the back of his hand. When no one is looking, she spits. Her tireless heart ticking. The skin around her eyes is creased like damp tissue paper. She touches it lightly, with two fingers. She births a child; his voice is shrill. He throws an apple, breaks a window. She grips his wrist too tightly, leaves fingerprints. She hears him in the next room, a man moving, her son. Once, she sees a patch of grass so green she wants to lie down on it more than anything. Her knuckles swell. She holds her book closer to her nose. She squints into distance. Bare trees bud, unfurl.

Eliza ended the reign of silence. One by one the prisoners were restored the privilege of speech so long as their speaking did not interrupt their handiwork or their studies. To one prisoner, whose moaning and weeping disturbed the other women, Eliza gave a cotton ragdoll.

"It belonged to my second son," she said. "He would want you to care for it." The doll's smile showed two teeth, stitched with black thread, and one of its small hands was chewed, but its new owner held it close. When the woman left her cell for work or meals she tucked the doll beneath the sheet on her cot, its orange yarn hair resting upon the pillow. Returning, she fed it crumbs, pressing them one at a time to the doll's embroidered mouth.

On each grim windowsill Eliza placed a terracotta pot of marigolds, chrysanthemums, or scarlet geraniums. From the ceilings she hung heavy lamps endowed with reflectors. She papered the walls with maps of New York, the United States, and Europe. On the Fourth of July she brought a basket of caramels. When she gained an assistant, Miss Georgiana Bruce, the gloom of the prison was all but eliminated, for Georgiana brought along her piano. It was installed in the classroom, and even the inmates were occasionally allowed to coax it in their riotous or rudimentary ways.

Five days a week Eliza gathered the women for lectures on American history, astronomy, geology, physiology, phrenology, and personal hygiene. "Education," said Eliza, "is one little step upward in the direction of the light."

For the lecture on phrenology, Eliza brought a drawing of a bald, androgynous head. In profile, its eye looked forward; a bit of paper was left white, indicating a glint. The eyebrow was too low and rested directly on the lashes. The nose was aquiline, and the lips curved in the suggestion of a smile. Beneath the rounded chin was a rash of shading that ran to the ear. The rounded part of the skull was divided into plots and parcels—this one a tiny square, this an oval, this an arched parallelogram along the crest. Each plot was labeled with its associated organ. Eliza tacked the drawing to the wall and raised her wooden pointer.

"The brain and the mind are one and the same," she said, and gave three sharp raps with the pointer. "As you can see, the skull is divided into thirty-seven regions, each reflecting the shape of the organ housed beneath." Her students stared, glassy-eyed. "Contained in the brain are all the secrets of personality—*why* we do the things we do and *how* we do them. Each aspect of character dwells within its own organ. Smaller organs are less powerful. The larger the organ, the more powerful. As our organs swell or shrink, so does their shell, the cranium." Still, the women stared. "A demonstration is in order? Ulrike Weiss, please stand."

Ulrike was a thief with a knack for embroidery. She was also a proficient pianist, almost a musical genius, but her behavior was erratic. One moment she calmly pulled a shining thread through a bit of cloth; the next she was pacing wildly, tearing at her careful stitches, the thread knotting and fraying as she muttered in German. She was regarded as insane.

"We all know how beautifully Ulrike plays the piano," said Eliza. "Some of us might plink our way through Beethoven every day for hours and never manage a melody quite the way Ulrike does." She pressed her middle and index fingers to each side of Ulrike's broad forehead, above the outer corners of her eyebrows. "This is region number thirty-four. It determines our ability to create or recreate a tune. And here," she said, sliding her fingers to Ulrike's temples, "is the organ of constructiveness, where our mechanical faculties are located. You can see how wide Ulrike's head is here. This combination explains her musical talent, not to mention her skill with a needle."

Eliza watched as the women began running their hands over their own skulls; Ulrike, restless, pulled away. Turning to the front of the room, Eliza was surprised to see the Chaplain leaning in the doorway.

"Well, well," he said. "We all recognize Ulrike's musical talent. She serves as a striking example, with that conveniently broad forehead. It lines up rather nicely."

"Science does have that tendency," said Eliza. "I understand you have a special interest in this subject. Shall we read another head while you're here?"

"I'd be delighted," the Chaplain said. "But let's make it more difficult so you might demonstrate your art more fully." From his breast pocket he pulled a blue silk handkerchief. He gave it a shake, like a magician completing a trick. "Why don't we do the next one blind?"

Eliza nodded and turned so the Chaplain could blindfold her. He smelled of soap and cedar, but she stopped her nose to his scent, breathing through her mouth as his hands tied the blindfold, tight. He took her hands, firmly, but without squeezing, and guided them to the level of the chosen woman's head. His thumbs pressed the centers of her palms, forcing her fingers to curl inwards, so she straightened them. Her hands were rigid when the Chaplain released them. She took a breath.

Eliza felt a warm and waxy film of grease. Her fingers were on the prisoner's eyelids, smooth and sticky. She slid each hand in unison, over the scruff of eyebrows to a smooth forehead, and soon her fingers met the woman's hairline. Eliza let them rest a moment, then traced a light circle and pushed them along the hairline, back into the twin pockets of a widow's peak, where she felt the slightest indentation, deeper on the right side than on the left.

"This woman has a deficit of mirth," she said. She slid her fingers through the prisoner's smooth, straight hair, allowing them to meet on the top of the skull, and there she felt the telltale bump of benevolence. "Pronounced benevolence." She slid her fingers down again and was surprised. On one side of the prisoner's head rose a bump more prominent than that of her own benevolence. This was the location of spirituality, and behind that, closer to the ear, the swell merged into sublimity, the organ for appreciating infinity and grandeur. She had not noticed these qualities in any of the prisoners. They were criminals, after all.

Eliza said nothing of these bumps but felt her pulse quicken. The head was flat in the region of conscientiousness, and there was the deficit of self-esteem she expected if the head belonged to Maria Giatti, and these she mentioned aloud. There were uneven swells above and behind the prisoner's ears—destructiveness and combativeness—organs that quickly gave way to violence, and these she felt she had to mention in order to prove her science. As her fingers met at the nape of the prisoner's neck, the Chaplain spoke.

"While you're blindfolded, what sort of sins is a person with this particular arrangement of bumps capable of?"

She let her fingers rest in the space between the muscles of the prisoner's neck.

"Destructiveness and combativeness are physical propensities," she said, "and coupled as they are with a lack of conscientiousness, this woman is likely to harm another—assault and battery, or even murder. However, considering her underdeveloped self-esteem, this woman may have been a victim of violence herself."

The Chaplain was silent.

"Would you like me to read another? Or could you remove the blindfold?" she asked, but she did not wait for his answer. She pulled the blindfold off, along with a couple of hairpins that fell to the floor, and Eliza felt her hair loosen, a few strands brushing her face. The Chaplain left the room without saying a word. Before Eliza stood Maria Giatti.

What can be learned from skulls aligned—sockets gaping, teeth chipped and angled, jeering and static? And from living skulls, with skin and eyes intact, tongues filling their caverns with heat and blood?

View this perfect specimen: a man, middle-aged, skin stretched and gleaming, hair like tendrils of a cloud. A blush within his pale skin. Twin swells for order and calculation. This skull is swollen with language—he speaks five.

This child's tiny skull, wide above the temples—he's filled with wonder! He runs along the drainage ditch and watches anthills swarm. He spins with open eyes, looking at the sun—he likes it when he falls. And this broad expanse behind his ears: he bludgeons birds to death and kicks down haystacks, throws crabapples through windows. Don't touch it; don't wake it. He might outgrow it.

And these, skulls heaped in a ditch, all with high cheekbones or wide foreheads or square jaws—push the dirt over them. Don't look too closely at these brittle goblets. A bit of dark flesh clinging still upon this jaw. Blood dried and darkening in a fracture. Don't look too closely: push the dirt, let them roll.

In her office Eliza slid a bulging volume from the shelf, its pages filled with the names of all the women in the prison and notes on their cases. Maria Giatti's name was printed in block lettering on a page near the middle of the book. Even with Eliza's established reliance on phrenology, she was surprised to see how well she had read Maria's head. When she turned the page, the writing changed to the tight, curlicued scrawl of the Chaplain, who spent one afternoon each week compiling information on the prisoners in hope of discovering the portals to their souls.

Maria had grown up an outsider, the child of Italians in an Irish neighborhood. Her father had worked in a shoe factory, but he had long since retired to the bottle. There was nothing written about her mother. Her entire life, Maria had been surrounded by drunkenness and brawling. She birthed a child, but the baby died of unknown causes. In the margin were penciled the words *Starvation?* and *Suffocation?* Of the infant's death there was no official record. There was no record, even, of her birth, which Maria claimed had taken place at home, in the kitchen. At this point another note: *Infection?*

Maria was eighteen and had been married three years when she killed her husband with a meat cleaver. She arrived at the prison two years ago with a matched set of black eyes, skin dappled with bruises, hair matted with blood. She walked in a hunch. When Eliza turned the page again, the sketches she had done of Maria's head fluttered out. She remembered stuffing them hastily into the book when a fight had broken out in the sewing room.

So the murder had been particularly gruesome. Although Maria's violent nature was evident in the shape of her skull, Eliza was surprised. The woman looked delicate, and Eliza had never seen her display even a hint of anger. Eliza shivered as her imagination conjured an image of Maria crusted in blood, her eyes swollen.

Eliza's own husband, an educated man, had once held her against the wall in a fit of anger, his tremendous fingers pressed around her neck. She had glimpsed his temper before, but not until this day had she been terrified, stunned at his capacity for rage and at her own in return. If she had been less shocked, she might have hit him once he released her, but instead she had wrapped her infant son in a blanket and taken her coat from the rack, prepared to leave.

"Where will you go?" her husband asked. He had fallen on the floor at her feet. He grasped one of her shoes. She had forgiven him, mostly.

She felt certain Maria had been provoked. On Eliza's fingertips lingered the memory of those unexpected bumps, spirituality and sublimity. Did the woman truly possess these exaggerated faculties? Eliza was obliged to answer yes. If Maria was a spiritual being, Eliza could use those traits to help the woman reform. Only her sense of justice needed unlocking.

Of the seventy-three convicts in Eliza's care, twenty-two could read and write, thirty could read but not write, and twenty-one were illiterate. In two-hour shifts, the women gathered fifteen at a time. The fully literate were paired with two who were not, and a tutoring session took place. "Like children in a little school," Eliza remarked to her assistant, and a woman at a nearby table looked up and glared. Eliza smiled at her.

Eliza and Georgiana occasionally worked with a prisoner alone in order to measure her progress. Maria was one of the thirty who could read but not write. Her letters and spelling were progressing slowly. She had yet to write a complete sentence unassisted. Eliza borrowed a Bible from the Chaplain's desk. It was covered in green leather with gilt-edged pages.

They read the story of Cain and Abel, alternating verses. Maria read first.

"And Cain talked with Abel his brother: and it came to pass, when they were in the field, that Cain rose up against Abel his brother, and slew him.

"And the Lord said unto Cain, Where is Abel thy brother? And he said, I know not: Am I my brother's keeper?

"And he said, What hast thou done? the voice of thy brother's blood crieth unto me from the ground."

Maria looked at Eliza with unblinking eyes. "Why are we reading this?" she asked.

"Do you believe in God, Maria?"

"I don't believe the Bible, if that's what you mean."

"Well, do you believe in God? Do you pray?" Maria stared.

"Honestly," Eliza said, "I've never believed in God myself. I don't know why I brought a Bible when I really just wanted to talk to you. Are you offended?" Still, Maria did not respond. "It's the story that interests me— the brothers. Have you ever talked with anyone about your husband?"

"Why are you asking me this?" Maria's voice was flat.

"Do you understand the difference between right and wrong?"

Maria looked away. "I know that you and Miss Georgiana are good," she said. Her hand was resting on the table, and Eliza covered it with her own, which was damp with sweat.

"Yesterday, when I was examining your head, I didn't mention everything I learned—you have another profound sentiment. I didn't reveal what I'd found because, well, I guess I was surprised. And I thought it might make you vulnerable somehow. The Chaplain was there. The other women."

Maria looked at her steadily.

"Here," said Eliza, lightly touching the side of Maria's head. "This is where your spirituality is located. And here," moving her fingers back, "is the organ of sublimity, your comprehension of infinity. Do you think about an afterlife?"

Maria pushed her chair back and stood. "Are we finished?"

In the kitchen, pots bubble over. Potato peels heap in the garbage bin. Stacks of dishes: these gleaming, these blackened. Hands are rubbed raw with steel wool. In the laundry, soap and steam. Hands are soggy and wrinkled. In the library, the spines of books line shelves like soldiers. Linen tape, waxed thread—a lucky prisoner repairs a loose cover, a broken spine, a fluttering page. Corridors gleam; mops glide. And in the sewing circle, needles flash, pulling taut an initial on a handkerchief, a flower on a tablecloth, a patch on an elbow, a loose pocket, a frayed cuff.

Eliza paced the courtyard. Around her, 800 cells were stacked four deep. Narrow windows faced off with staccato regularity. She imagined the prisoners within the walls, standing on tip-toe to look onto this scene, where she was crunching gravel beneath her shoes. This was the men's courtyard. She could almost smell their sweat, their excrement. Inside, the men were working—hammering soles onto shoes. Rolling leaves into cigars. Building chairs and tables with their coarse hands.

Her husband's hands were like that, coarse and chapped from days spent working winter fields. Once, when he had touched her naked breast, she had called him a goblin. He hadn't laughed but had scraped her skin with a torn fingernail, had squeezed her nipple, hard. But he was far away now. She hadn't had a letter in a month.

Maria's hands were soft—softer than Eliza's, and much smaller. They were the hands of a child. An elegant, aristocratic child, bathed in rose oil and dusted with talcum. It was incredible, Eliza thought, that those hands were attached to such a wild creature. Violence, she thought, seemed mismatched in one who grasped the concept of infinity.

Eliza closed her eyes and focused on the darkness of her inner eyelids. It was a shallow space, between lens and lid, but it looked like an endless, buzzing dark. It was the only eternity she could imagine. The wind blew through the courtyard with a quiet moan. The prison, Eliza thought, was like a tremendous woman, holding her children close, Eliza included.

Soft mounds of cloth lay about the women's ankles, never diminishing. The women sat in straight-backed chairs around a patch of light that fell on the floor from the window. Georgiana sat at a table near the door with her own embroidery—a nightgown for her sister. The women talked while they sewed but were forbidden to speak of their crimes. They spoke of children they'd left in the world and sometimes of the morning's lecture, but usually they dwelt on what they wanted from the outside. In winter, piping-hot gingerbread and lavender soap. In spring, a new pair of stockings. Sometimes it was a long, steamy bath or a vial of perfume. Always it was a man.

For two days after her talk with Eliza, Maria had kept silent. The women were accustomed to her sulks—she had once gone two weeks without saying a word—but this time was different. She was constantly losing the thread from her needle, sighing and scuffing her shoes beneath her chair. When she managed to keep the needle threaded, she pulled so tightly the needle laid a groove in her thumb.

The woman who sat beside Maria dragged her chair away. On Maria's other side sat Gretchen Felter, who, years ago, had attacked a keeper with a hand-fashioned knife and was beaten into submission with a cane. Gretchen made a show of shoving Maria's chair out of the circle and stepping indelicately on her foot.

With a half inch of sloppy stitches, Maria sewed her hand to the shirt she was mending. The hem of the shirt was red with blood, clinging to the skin between thumb and finger.

It was Gretchen who noticed. "Hey," she said. "Stop that. Stop that now." She reached for the shirt, but Maria pulled away. "What are you doing?"

Maria raised her needle high, pulling the thread taut, her face expressionless, her eyes wide. Georgiana stumbled around the circle of chairs, but before she could reach Maria, Gretchen struck Maria's cheek with the back of her hand. Maria focused on Gretchen as if she'd never seen her before, her eyes narrowed.

"Lord Jesus and the angels! What is wrong with you?" Gretchen said.

Georgiana grasped Maria's elbow and pulled her roughly to her feet. On the way out of the room, Maria faltered and pressed her hand to the doorframe to steady herself, leaving behind a smeared red handprint.

Eliza heard about the incident but was busy in the kitchen, where one woman had pushed a pot of boiling water onto another, scalding her feet. Both women were hysterical. Eliza hated punishing her women, but the offender was hung from her wrists for half an hour and placed in confinement for a week.

With a terrible headache, Eliza closed her office door. She took out a book she was in the process of editing, about the criminal mind, but her eyes drifted to the window, a square of blue with black birds flying across it.

Once, Eliza had dropped a spoon while her husband was reading. There was a clatter of silver on stone and he stood, red-faced and looming, enraged by the noise. He left the room. And once, he stubbed his toe, and as he hopped across the floor, grimacing, she had laughed. He slapped her across the cheek. One Sunday, after church, which she attended only for his benefit, she looked too long at a neighbor's wife who was wearing a new Sunday dress. The woman's waist was a slender stalk, the buttons precise, and a bit of lace grazed her chin as she descended the steps from the church. Eliza's husband pulled her firmly by the elbow. "You're staring," he said, squeezing her arm. When he held the babies, they cried. And when her son, the one who lived, was old enough to walk, the boy had taken to hiding in her skirt when his father entered the room. She remembered a hailstorm that battered the crops, and though it had nothing to do with her, her husband had swept her books across the table and onto the floor; he slammed doors.

She filled too hot a bath for him. He didn't check the water—he never did—but stepped in quickly and lost his balance. He wasn't scalded, just startled, but he flung the door open—his naked skin flushed, his penis dangling. There was dirt beneath his fingernails, his skin dappled with sunspots, veins raised like scars. There was the flicker of the hearth and their two shadows, which moved like tortured puppets on the wall. And then his face was so close to hers, so boiled red, a fleck of spittle, flared nostrils. His thumb pressed between her jaw and ear, his palm pushed at her throat. There was no longer a windblown house, a room with a hearth. Only the pressure around her neck, her toes tipping the floor, and his hot breath, the pulse in his temple, his cavernous mouth.

She dropped her eyes. He let her go.

The Chaplain's office was orderly: a tin cup of pencils and an African violet blooming on the windowsill. He sat straight in his armless chair, both elbows propped upon the desk. Eliza found his office surprisingly peaceful compared to her own, where papers were always strewn and the wastebasket perpetually overflowed with crumpled pages. The ivy plant on her windowsill had recently withered, the tips of its leaves crinkled and browned. She had dosed it with fertilizer Georgiana had concocted from coffee grounds and potato peels, but the plant didn't seem to be reviving.

"Yes?" the Chaplain said, looking up from his work.

"I'd like to talk about Maria Giatti," Eliza said, stepping closer. "She isn't well. Have you spoken with her?"

He had not. There was a second chair, and he offered it to Eliza with a tight-lipped smile.

"I left something out when I did my reading the other day. Something that might be of interest to you."

"I doubt that anything you learned from the topography of a battered woman's skull will be of interest to me. You got lucky, Mrs. Farnham."

"You know I find your methods antiquated, but if you're successful using them, I won't call it luck."

"You recognized her by her hair. I should've known you'd recognize the contours of *that* head, the way you're always watching her."

Eliza's scalp prickled. "What do you mean?"

He turned and looked directly at her. She held his gaze but felt a flush creep up her neck.

"Never mind," she said. "I thought this was something we could work on together, but clearly I was wrong." She stood.

"Mrs. Farnham," the Chaplain said, "only God can fix them."

To get to California you could take a wagon and likely perish in a swollen river or die of fever on the dried-up prairie. Or you could sail, south and south, until you reached Cape Horn, with winds blowing you ever nearer your death, and then, rounding the Cape, you had to sail north just as long. Still, if Eli-za ever went, she'd take this second route. She'd seen enough of prairies, and she'd see mountains once she reached California—if she reached it. If not, at least she'd see the strange birds that reportedly flew around the Cape. She'd see tremendous swimming turtles and hear sea lions bellow. They'd dock at ports where people spoke as if singing, in burbling words she couldn't understand. Yes, if Eliza went to California, she would sail.

Early the next morning Eliza found Maria sleeping, face to the wall, her left hand wrapped in gauze. Eliza hooked her fingers through the cell door and watched Maria's chest rise and fall. Maria's hair had come loose from its plait and was sprawled across her pillowcase. She was talking in her sleep. Eliza leaned her head against the cool metal, trying to decode the sleeper's mumbled words.

"Snowdrops," she thought she heard. "There's a penny." It was nonsense but lovely. Maybe Maria was dreaming of an afterlife. She studied Maria's profile, the curve of her hip. The girl had slept in her boots. Behind Eliza, in another cell, a prisoner spit the word *whore*. Eliza had already watched too long.

Maria did not wake at the sound of her cell door opening. At the foot of the bed Eliza saw a rumpled sheet of paper. Maria had been practicing her writing. A row of almost perfect capitals stretched across the page. A wobbly K was crossed out.

"Maria," she said. She stretched a hand to Maria's shoulder and shook her, lightly. "I need to talk to you."

Maria put her gauze-wrapped hand over her ear, her elbow jutting awkwardly upward.

"I'm busy," she said, and she did not turn.

Eliza studied Maria's elbow. It was dry and cracked. "Busy?" she said. Maria pressed her hand tighter over her ear. "With what?" Eliza leaned down and pried Maria's hand from her ear.

"Can't you see I'm injured?" Maria said. She cradled her bandaged hand with her whole one.

"That's what I want to talk to you about. What's bothering you? You did this to yourself."

Maria pulled her pillow over her face as if threatening to smother herself. Eliza pulled it away. Maria sat up. She looked like a child, with her boots hanging over the edge of her cot, her knobby elbows, her clear eyes looking up at Eliza, squinting a little. Eliza sat down beside her.

"What if . . ." Eliza said. "Do you think you could get better? If we worked very hard?"

Maria tipped her head to the side, mockingly. "Am I sick?" she said. "I feel all right, besides my hand."

"I think so. I think you're sick—not bad. Not evil." She patted Maria's knee. "I could take you to California." She hadn't planned to say it, but once the words were out, they just kept coming. "Do you know where that is? My husband is there—he says it's beautiful. He says you can stand atop a cliff and see for miles across the sea, which is greener there. He says it isn't a place for a woman. But I think it is. I think it's just the place for a woman, if she is strong enough—and brave."

"The Chaplain says I'll never get out of here," Maria said. "Not until I die."

"Well, the Chaplain and I have different ideas."

"California," said Maria flatly.

"Listen to this." Eliza opened the book she had brought. She had marked a passage, and she followed along with her finger as she read. "Those who take the trouble to refer to any considerable number of cases of murder will be struck by the remarkable fact that the homicidal is almost invariably accompanied by the suicidal tendency; and hence, that persons who are in the state of mind which renders them capable of attempting the destruction of a fellow-creature are usually, at the same time, desirous of self-destruction."

Maria's face was smooth and pale, impassive as a teacup.

"You don't understand?"

Maria shook her head.

"It says that someone who has killed another person probably despises herself, probably wishes to harm herself as well. . . . Is that why you sewed through your own hand? To punish yourself?"

"I just wasn't paying attention," Maria said. "I didn't do it on purpose."

"You must have felt it."

"No. I didn't."

"Do you feel bad about what happened with your husband? Is that why?"

Maria shifted away from her. "Look," Maria said, pulling her hair tight against the sides of her head. "Can't you see that?" She ran her fingers through her hair, parting it to show Eliza more of her scalp. "Those are scars," she said. "Couldn't you tell in your examination?"

Eliza touched Maria's head with the tips of her fingers, parting the hair as Maria had done. The skin was shiny and white. Eliza found the familiar prominence she had noted earlier in the week—the organ of spirituality. The bone was thicker where Maria's skull had healed poorly, and above that was a barbed scar where her skin had been surgically stitched together.

Eliza pulled her hands away and wiped them on her skirt. Maria held her gaze.

"I don't feel bad about my husband," Maria said. "He got what was coming to him. He'd have done the same to me if I'd let him. If he'd had another minute. He came close plenty of times."

At the end of the corridor the door slid open and Chaplain Luckey made his way toward them, coughing lightly.

"Thought I might find you here," Luckey said. "You haven't been here all night, have you?"

"What do you want?" Eliza asked. Maria lay down on her cot and covered her face with her hands.

"You're late for the meeting," he said. He was smiling. He put out his hand to help her up. "The board is waiting—it's time for you to account for yourself." She had forgotten—her monthly review.

She went with him, looking once over her shoulder as she left the cell. Maria lay on her cot, pulling at her bandage with her teeth. The Chaplain held the door. Eliza saw the outer corridor, wider and brighter. Maria's skull had been sculpted, not by God and not by her organs. She was cooling metal now. She was quicklime, caustic and gusted, still settling. Eliza stepped into the corridor.

VICTORIA PIER, MONTREAL HARBOR

When I walk at the pier, I remember walking with Robert before he left for France, his hand in mine always a little sweaty, even in winter. There was no clock tower then but instead fishing boats, and the passenger ferry that we never took, with its many windows and decks, and men in straw hats, leaning on their elbows and smoking pipes, and women holding children's hands or else squinting at books held between licked forefingers and thumbs. *Books or children*, everyone said. *A woman must choose.* I don't remember choosing books, but they are good company to me most days.

It is winter again, and great slabs of ice jostle on the surface of the river, shoving as if to corrode each other. But this is the beauty of winter—to slow us down, to make something solid of us, and then break us down again into liquid, vaporous beings.

The city built the clock for sailors who died in the war, but they never got around to filling the tower with bells, and so it ticks but doesn't sing. The boats dock farther upriver now, by the grain elevators, and on winter mornings such as this, it's just me here, alone, breathing into my hands.

PAPYRUS OF THE YELLOW-THROATED WARBLER

Here begin the chapters of the coming forth by day.
We were kneeling on the driveway of our rental house, our first house together, and our last. We were looking at a dead bird—small, yellow-throated and intact, tiny talons curled.

You said a bird's heart beats much faster than a human heart. Its blood races through every millimeter of its body in no time at all.

I suggested we mummify the little thing—remove its brain, a brain being useless in the Egyptian afterlife. But I got it wrong. I said the heart, too, would have to go.

No, no, you said. You shook your head. Not the heart. The heart is the only organ that stays. The heart rules the soul and the intellect. It goes with the body to the afterlife so it can be weighed against the feather. A heavy heart is a guilty heart, and it gets eaten by Ammut, the half-crocodile, half-hippopotamus god.

No heart is lighter than a feather, I said.

Your eyes were unblinking, your beautiful eyes, a freckle in each iris. Your eyes, so light brown they could almost be called yellow. I blinked first.

Okay, you said, nudging the bird with your index finger.

For the time being, we wrapped it in a rumpled tissue you found in your pocket.

It's perfectly clean, you said, smoothing it out. It was just in case you needed it.

Let me do all the things one does on the earth, such as walking hither and thither.

The Egyptian *Book of the Dead* is also known as *Spells for Coming or Going Forth by Day*. It is full of prayers, praise hymns, instructions, and pleas: for a mouth, for breath, to prevent rotting, to maintain or regain control of one's legs, to retain one's heart.

In the afterlife the heart is in continual danger of being snatched.

How, then, after all these prayers, with heart and mouth and breath intact, with legs that walk and bend and grow sore with use—how is the afterlife different from the present life? The Egyptian underworld seems to run parallel to the overworld, a separate but similar village, located beneath the soil but above the molten core.

But keep reading, you would say. There are prayers for avoiding work, for turning into a sparrow or a heron or a hawk, for turning into a water lily.

One must work in the afterlife? Cutting and cultivating the field of reeds? And who would want to be a water lily? A flower: tall and bright and beautiful, but inanimate? Your stem so long, so tangled, so far from your plumage, and all of you nourished by pond muck?

Come forth by day. Go forth by day. There are no prayers for night.

Offerings include: cakes and ale, barley-wheat, mud bricks, reeds.

Our rental house was on the lake, fronted by cedars that swarmed with mosquitoes. It was shake-shingled, painted gray and peeling. The back of the house was all glass—windows and sliding doors looked across the sand to the water. The lake was gray that day. It was often gray, even during summer. It was July; it must have been nine o' clock, but the sun hadn't set. You unlocked the front door and reached down to slap a mosquito off the back of your knee. You smashed it mid-bite and smeared blood across your skin.

I am silent.
From the right side of the heart, blood comes forth into the lungs. From the lungs, blood goes forth to the rest of the body. All day and night, the blood goes forth.

Thy right eye is like the Sektet Boat, thy left eye is like the Atet Boat.
For the mummification you covered the kitchen table with typing paper. You cut the bird's skull open with a scalpel I never knew you had. The blade was fresh. You scooped the brain out with a teaspoon, like seeds from a melon.

Useless brain, I said.
I touched your temple with my fingers, but you were busy. You brushed my hand away.

You sliced along the bird's sternum.
Why don't you prepare the bandages? you said.
I got up from the table. It was like a hospital in our kitchen—like a hospital and like a morgue. The ugly lamp hung from a chain above the table. Moths circled. Hospital. Morgue. Temple. Prison. You dropped the brain into the trash.

In town, fifteen miles north, drunks were staggering through the streets. Teenagers were necking at the swimming beach, clammy-skinned, their heads filled with cricket chirps. Cars drove up Jefferson, windows rolled down. Middle-aged couples strolled, licking ice cream cones and doling out bite-sized pieces of fudge to their grubby children, who dropped lumps of chewing gum on the sidewalk. At that very moment, tee shirt vendors were turning out shop lights and locking doors, stepping into the night, stretching and sighing.

You and I agreed: We hated candy apples, ice cream, fudge, and caramel corn. We hated fingernail polish and lipstick; suntans; and big, bright, expensive sneakers. We hated golf pants and diamond rings.

But I have always liked the color of streetlight on a summer night. I lie awake and listen for the rising and falling of music as a car passes. When we met— remember? I lived above the shops in town, where I heard laughter and whistling and glasses clinking at all hours. Once in a while, a cigarette, or the chance of an unexpected whisper in my ear—the way the hair on my arms rises, the three little bones in my ear vibrate, the lips of the whisperer so close but not touching me.

Dedication: hair, lips, teeth, belly, flesh, trunk, fingers, breast, backbone, throat.

A note on the Papyrus of Hunefer: On his way to the afterlife, Hunefer is clothed in semi-translucent white. The outline of his thin, straight legs is evident through the gown. Like many Egyptians depicted on papyrus, Hunefer is androgynous but for his black goatee. He is both stiff and graceful, looking ahead, holding the hand of Inpu, the jackal god. Hunefer's feet, face, and hands are drawn in profile, but his chest and shoulders face forward, like a Barbie doll gone wrong, its shoulders twisted out of line by an older sibling or a teething baby.

Hunefer, I tell you: There is no turning back. The jackal god sees through your clothes, through your skin. Your heart, after all, is no longer beating inside your chest but is even now being lowered to the scales.

Crouched beside the scales sits Ammut: bone eater, swallower, devourer of the dead. With the hind quarters of a hippopotamus and the snout of a crocodile, she can't run very fast. Her legs are too stubby. No hunting for Ammut. She is the dog of the underworld, waiting for table scraps or rawhide, waiting for your heart. It is delivered directly to her mouth.

I am a sparrow. I am a sparrow. I am a scorpion.

Since early June, I had been taking long walks in the dark. Each night, fires burned along the beach, and there were always boys drinking beer. Sometimes they threw bottles into the flames. Once I watched a boy piss on the fire to put it out—all acrid, hissing steam. His friends were gone. He was the last one. He didn't see me standing at the water's edge, watching. He finished and lay down on the sand, outside the ring of rocks and stumps on which the boys usually sat. He stretched out on his back and looked up at the stars and the dwindling column of smoke. I walked on.

I have dipped and washed and buried the inside parts. I have dug them up.

Buried in hot sand, a body dries quickly, though not as quickly as flesh rubbed with natron, a kind of salty soda-ash. Natron desiccates the flesh, which is then opened, the organs removed. The brain is crushed and drained through the nostrils. The body is wrapped and wrapped and tucked away. But sand and natron are not the only ways. There is ice. There is the density and acid of the peat bog.

It is air and water that damage us. All our lives we need them, but in death we are defenseless against their swarms.

Adze, chisel, little finger: open my mouth.

You pried the bird's chest open with your scalpel while I dipped linen strips in flour paste. You were wearing your glasses. They slipped down your nose and cast shadows across your cheekbones.

You already knew about Jonah. You said you'd forgive me.

You pulled out little, indistinguishable viscera.

I asked if you would bury them with the mummy, in jars.

You didn't even nod.

You knew about Jonah. You knew I had gone with him, once or twice, to the garden shack where he slept on a cot. He didn't have electricity, but he had a bowl of peaches on a rough table. He had half a bottle of red wine. He had flat, brown, thickly callused feet. He had a frayed red rug that needed to be laundered. You didn't want to know more. You said you'd forgive me, but I didn't want to be forgiven.

◆◆◆

*I have not caught fish with bait made of the bodies of the
same kind of fish.*

No heart is lighter than a feather, even if the heart
is small and the feather large. The average adult heart
weighs between nine and eleven ounces, surprisingly light,
yet heavier, certainly, than the average ostrich feather. A
heart—for all that muscle and protein, the ventricles and
atria and various valves, the four chambers still heavy
with blood—has the heft of two cups of hazelnuts, or a
stick and a half of butter.

Keep from me the stinking bones.

Where are you now? Sitting at a desk, surrounded by
books, a half-full glass of water condensing on a coaster
within your reach? You take methodical sips. You run
your fingers through your hair. It's short, I'm sure. Or
even shaved, so you don't have to worry about it. I loved
that about you—the minimalism: the black coffee, the
undressed salad, the perfectly trimmed nails. You lean
close to the copy of a papyrus pressed beneath a sheet of
glass. You pause and take off your glasses to polish the
lenses with the cloth you keep folded in your pocket.

I have not tampered with the plumb bob of the balance.

It was Hippocrates who taught us that the heart only
beats. The heart is mere battery while the brain is the intellect, personality, emotion, and soul. The brain became
separate and superior to the body. The brain is where in-
tangibles pulse: guilt, god, epiphany. And these? Magnetic
fields flickering against the parietal temporal lobe.

I am content when I breathe his odor.

Jonah is a bartender, and a kayak guide on the
lake. Paddle with a rhythm, he says. Rock a little. Sit
up straight. He points out the shipwreck and how the
buoy marks the channel. In September, he weatherizes
summer homes. In December, he plays hockey with a
broom. He runs a snow blower, clears the sidewalk in

front of the restaurant with goats on the roof. He eats dandelion greens, almonds and lentils, dried fruit, day-old bagels. In the morning he sits on the step in the sun. The mosquitoes lay low when the sun is hot. Once, he let me peel a callus from the bottom of his foot.

Heart scarab, dung beetle, quiet my heart.

In ancient Egypt the sun was a dung ball rolled across the sky each day by Khperi, god of the rising sun—a dung beetle. Day after day, the beetle rolled its dung across the sky.

I have not stopped the flow of water.

Or I wanted to be forgiven, but I didn't want you to take me back. I didn't want you to kiss my closed eyelids. I didn't want to watch your chest rise and fall while you slept beneath our cheap muslin sheets. I didn't want to lie beside you, watching the sky through the bare window, listening to you breathe, until the leaves browned and fell and the trees stood bare, and the lake grew a new crust, and still the sheet over your chest rose and fell.

The bird didn't make it. When you pulled out the viscera the bones gave way. The body was empty and delicate and crushed, but you said: Do you want to see the heart? It might be lighter than a feather. It's very small.

You held it out for me to see and pulled the chest open with the tip of scalpel. I leaned in. It was tiny, severed, just sitting in there, like a raisin.

Even as Jonah traced my clavicle with a single finger, and the hair on my arms rose, I sat perfectly still, and even then, I thought of you—washing your hands and drying them, so slowly, then unrolling the papyrus onto your desk. Setting your pen down and shaking your hand to keep it from cramping. The way you sometimes mutter when you write.

Jonah said, Relax.

The lake stone I gave you, smooth and pale: your heart scarab, your paperweight. How you wanted, more than anything, to be the lake.

UNTIL WE SEE SIGNS
AND WONDERS

By the time I met him, Edgar was already a little bit famous. He was in his early thirties, and it had been years since the Little People stopped speaking with him. The animals that had kept him company in his youth also kept their distance, but he had a wife and two children, and his reputation as a medical clairvoyant was spreading across the south. He'd even been written up in the *New York Times*, although they called him illiterate, which wasn't true. Edgar could read just fine, although he often used an unconventional method, laying his head upon a book, closing his eyes, and absorbing the contents of the pages straight into his brain as if through osmosis. He could recite almost every word of a book he read in this manner despite that it was—*is*—impossible. I didn't believe a word of it.

I was born and raised in Bowling Green, Kentucky, which is considered a city round those parts, but I had gone north, to Chicago, for college. I wanted smokestacks, ironworks, and trains rattling between tall buildings. I was convinced that industry was the key to the future. My Pops and Mama never understood why I didn't just go to Western like everyone I grew up with—the Hilltop, they called it—or to Emory if I was so ambitious. Emory was a fine Southern institution. Plenty of other greasy bones around there, Mama said. Greasy bones was what she called ambitious folks. But the Yankee bug bit hard, drained my Southern blood like a tick, and infected me with what Mama called *ideers*. Still, by the time I finished journalism school, in spring of 1910, I was a little homesick. I wrote a letter, sent a few clips, and lined up a spot covering the births, deaths, and marriages beat back at the *Bowling Green Daily News*.

I hitched a ride with a man from the *Sun Times* who had some story to cover down south. When we got close to Bowling Green, where the hills began to roll and the mist drifted up from the low spots, I spotted the first tobacco barn with its black creosote boards, and I actually asked the driver to pull over so I could get out and breathe a minute. "Carsick?" he asked, but I just pushed open my door and ran into the field, dew darkening my shoes, arms out wide, and I let out a shout I hadn't even felt brewing. I was glad to be home.

The thing about the South is that it is full of superstitions, ghost stories, and magic. Even though I had missed those green hills and misty hollers, the smoky cafes where they serve coffee with the spoon sitting in the cup, and even the sound of the fiddles sawing in a lot out behind the church—even if I am a Southerner in my heart—I do not believe in ghosts. I am not superstitious. And God doesn't get off the hook, either, being just another ghost.

Science! Industry! At the bar after work, I made loud, bourbon-fueled pronouncements. I'd push my chair back and do a bit of proselytizing. Finger-in-the-air stuff. Once or twice I even ranted in the newsroom, and my fellow journalists stopped typing and looked up, slack-jawed, pausing in their stories about the upcoming city council elections or the price of salt pork, the new program in home economics at the college. They looked up, but they weren't listening so much as marveling. At the confidence of youth. The certainty of knowledge. I was obnoxious.

Science! Industry! I loved all things steel and plastic. I loved modern medicine. To hell with this backwoods herbal-remedy hokum. To hell with their palm reading, their ghost stories, their iridology, which took place on the edge of town in a tiny cabin where people waited all day for the practitioner to look deep into their eyes and tell them what ailed them. Lined up on the porch, the "patients" clutched little sacks of tobacco or bundles of furry mullein leaves. These were payments for the "doctor." They also paid with cornmeal, sugar, cured bacon, and moonshine, and they waited and waited for that little old man to look into their eyes and tell them, based on some dot in their iris, if they had kidney disease or were pregnant or had cancer or melancholy. He prescribed nettle tea and raspberry leaves, cold compresses and lard ointments. Backwoods quackery, I called it, and I wrote an article about it, too.

Somehow, I had a girl. Merry Miller was studying biology on the Hilltop. She wanted to be a doctor and was serving as a research assistant in one of the labs. Her father was a professor of history, but despite her parents' insistence on education, they didn't encourage her medical aspirations. Merry often mimicked her mother, speaking in a nasal voice: "Oh, Merry! If you would just make some *effort!* Don't you want to meet a *nice* man and get married like your sister?"

Her sister, Michael Ann, had married a dentist and lived in a large house with a wraparound porch. Michael Ann was a local beauty, a charming, graceful debutante. She had started a local soup kitchen that I had once featured in the paper, but she had recently birthed her first child, a premature boy, so for the time being, the soup kitchen had to go on without her.

I was not what Merry's parents considered a "nice man." They were civil enough to my face, but Merry reported that they complained about my tattered clothing and my *uppityness.* They were, however, glad to see her going out in the evenings to someplace other than the lab, and I think she liked the rebelliousness of dating someone her parents didn't much care for. I took her to local dances, but we never danced. We sat at a table in the corner, sipping punch, hashing out what Bowling Green needed to really put it on the map, to bring it into the future: a new hospital, a better library, a decent streetcar, liquor on Sundays, and no more churches. Once in a while, I took her to the bar, and she listened to me rant—the liquor really brought it out. Together we would teach these hicks. We'd bring this gorgeous, backward place into the glassy, gleaming twentieth century.

And then I met Edgar.

In addition to covering births, deaths, and marriages, my editor allowed me to write the occasional "community interest" article. As a vigilante for progress, I often wrote about people or businesses that seemed opposed to it, and when I saw a flyer for one of Edgar Cayce's psychic readings, tacked to the board outside the post office, I took the bait.

TONIGHT! HEALER AND
PSYCHIC COUNSELOR EDGAR CAYCE!

BRING YOUR AILMENTS TO MR. CAYCE:
PROPHET, PSYCHIC, AND HEALER!
MR. CAYCE WILL OFFER DIAGNOSES AND
USEFUL TREATMENT METHODS!

MR. CAYCE IS A CHRISTIAN MAN WITH
GOD-GIVEN VISION TO HELP THE SICK!

DON'T MISS THIS INCREDIBLE
OPPORTUNITY FOR HEALING!

Tiny grandmothers with rheumatic claws. Mothers with sick children. Husbands with back pains, worried about their jobs, their ailing farm animals, the tobacco crop. All the saddest and most vulnerable of Bowling Green, and here was this "psychic," ready to fleece them. It was my civic duty to expose him.

◆◆◆

Edgar Cayce had wide, deeply shadowed eyes. It looked as if he had not slept in days. His hair was fair and receding, but his face was boyish, with fleshy lips and large ears. He wore a woolen suit with a three-button vest, a pocket square and watch. When he smiled, he did not look like a charlatan but rather like a friend. When I introduced myself before the show, he shook my hand firmly.

"Pleased to meet you, Mr. Reilly."

"Why would it please you?" I said. "I intend to reveal you as a quack and a swindler."

"Goodness, my man," he laughed. "I, too, disbelieved it. But it's all quite out of my control. In any case, I hope you'll find the evening of interest."

I chose a front-row seat. Edgar came onstage with a plain woman he introduced as his wife and assistant. The theater was very quiet. Edgar explained that he would begin with a long-distance reading, a letter sent to him from New York. He held the envelope up to show us that it was sealed, the stamp canceled—an easy enough forgery, I thought, the ruse of a steamed-open envelope. He gestured to his wife, who stepped to the front of the stage.

"Mr. Cayce will now put himself in a trance," said Mrs. Cayce. She looked from one side of the theater to the other. She held her hands folded in front of her. "It is not in his body that the answers lie but rather in his soul, as they are in yours. It is his soul that understands the language of the universe. It is his soul that knows where to look."

Edgar lay down on a long, velvet-covered sofa, removed his shoes, and rested his feet on the other end of the sofa. He closed his eyes and folded his hands lightly over the buttons of his vest. His wife cut open the envelope with a penknife and unfolded the letter. She read it aloud.

Dear Mr. Cayce,

I am writing on behalf of my mother, who is too ill to write, although she would not write to you even if she could because she does not believe in psychic powers, or even in the afterlife, but I know that she is wrong. I hope you will be able to help her.

For two years, my mother's health has steadily declined. The doctor has seen her many times, but nothing he has done has helped. It all began when she woke up one morning and discovered her eyes were nearly swollen shut, and the swelling reached halfway down her cheeks and across the bridge of her nose. Other than the swelling, she felt fine, and by the time she went to bed at night she looked almost normal, but every morning the swelling had returned. Each night, she told herself she was better, and each morning she found it was not so. Her feet, ankles, and fingers were also swollen, and she had to remove her wedding band because it was too tight. The doctor said it was allergies, although at the time she was 47 years old and had never before suffered allergies.

The swelling began to abate around the time that the rash developed. It was worst where her clothes pressed most tightly to her skin—wrists, hip bones, ankles. At her ankles, it spread up her shins and grew fiercely red and bumpy. The doctor prescribed a salve and begged her not to scratch, but she scratched furiously, and her legs were soon covered with bloody scabs that oozed and grew infected.

While Mrs. Cayce read the letter, Edgar appeared to be asleep. The letter continued on to describe how the poor woman eventually found herself bedridden and unrecognizable, her body ballooned so she could not even bend her arms at the elbows, her skin covered with festering scabs.

Mrs. Cayce reached the end of the letter and, on the sofa, Edgar's jaw fell open as if to release some moth or butterfly, but instead, his voice came out. He sounded different from when he was awake. A believer would have said he spoke with the voice of his spirit and not the voice of his body, which was shallow as a paper doll.

"Your mother is suffering a severe allergic reaction,"
he said. "She is allergic to food additives and dyes. She
is also diabetic. She must avoid artificially colored foods,
preservatives, and especially sugar."

Mrs. Cayce scribbled furiously in a notebook. The
instructions would be mailed to the letter writer, which
seemed inefficient, prolonging the woman's suffering
should his cure somehow work. And how were we, the
audience, to know if the diagnosis was correct or the
treatment effective? It was all highly unsatisfying.

He did two more long-distance readings, one of them
by telephone, which was more efficient but no more
convincing. He took a break after the long-distance
readings, bringing himself out of the trance with a little
snort, like a person with sleep apnea when their breath
finally reasserts itself. He sat up on the sofa and stretched.

"I'd like to tell you about how I discovered my
strange ability," he said. He spoke again in his waking
voice, less certain, with a bit of a rasp. He told us how,
only a few years back, he had been working as an
insurance salesman for his father's business. He had
done moderately well, and his family had a comfortable
life, but he did not find the work particularly satisfying.
He felt that God had something more in mind for him,
but he had not yet discovered what it was. Then he and
his wife had a second child, a boy, but the child was born
sickly and died after only a couple of months.

At this point, Mrs. Cayce sat down on the sofa and
looked at her hands. Edgar patted her knee and went on.
He said that in the months after his son's death, he had
completely lost his voice. He would open his mouth to
speak, and nothing would come out—neither scratch nor
syllable. He could whisper, he said, because whispering
did not require the vibration of the vocal cords. His
vocal cords, it seemed, were gummed into place, unable
to vibrate, and this went on for well over a year. He was
forced to quit selling insurance and began working as
a studio photographer, taking pictures of babies and
families and couples on their wedding days. He gestured

a lot, he said, and he smiled. He learned to communicate with his body, with his face, and people seemed strangely at ease with a whispering photographer. His new line of work allowed him to stay in town with his wife and their remaining son, and soon his wife was pregnant again. She gave birth to another boy, who was now three years old, healthy and strong.

Despite his enjoyment of photography, he wondered if he would ever speak again. Where had his voice gone? So when he heard of a traveling hypnotist, a man who could cure addictions and find answers to difficult questions, he visited the man, who put him in a trance during which Edgar spoke normally, but when Edgar awoke, his voice was gone once again. Could it be a psychological ailment? Perhaps something to do with grief over his lost son? The hypnotist suggested that Edgar go into a trance again and he, the hypnotist, would ask Edgar to diagnose himself. Perhaps, if it were a psychological ailment, his unconscious mind would give up the answers when his conscious mind was asleep.

Beyond all expectation, it worked. In the trance, Edgar told the hypnotist that his voice box was not receiving enough blood. The answer was to simply direct more blood to his throat. And with that Edgar began to flush at the neck, growing quite red, although his face and hands remained pale. The hypnotist touched Edgar's throat and found that it was hot. He commanded Edgar to awake, but first Edgar coughed, pulled his handkerchief from his pocket, and spit into it a wad of thick, disgusting phlegm. "The treatment is complete," he said, fully awake now, clutching the damp, wadded-up handkerchief, and sure enough, he was healed.

The story did not make a believer of me, but the article I wrote was not the one I had planned. Although I still believed wholeheartedly that Edgar was a con, I liked him—a fatal flaw in a journalist, letting feelings influence his work—but at that point I was unable to rake the muck I suspected. I concluded my article with an honest assessment.

Cayce's April 2nd performance was steeped in flimsy magic and rambling tales. His apparent humility, however, adds convincing authenticity to the act. Perhaps Cayce is himself convinced of the truth of his visions, of his ability to read the so-called "Akashic Record," which he describes as "the recorded history of our souls in the universe." If so, this is the most brilliant aspect of his con: by conning even himself, he makes it exceedingly difficult to discover his ploy.

Merry read that article aloud, in a clear, practiced voice. It was a Sunday afternoon, and I was on the swing on Michael Ann's porch. Merry had the newspaper folded over in her hands and was pacing while she read, though the porch was only wide enough to allow three or four steps in either direction. Michael Ann sat in a wicker chair with her baby swaddled on her lap. She was squinting and making kissy faces at the child, only half listening.

"The Akashic Record," Merry said, when she was done. "Is that like a layer of the atmosphere? A scrim of swirling spirits? I wonder if it blocks the sun on days when many people die, like during wars. I wonder if it gets denser as time progresses. I think Dante might have drawn it. Or was it Hieronymus Bosch?"

"And maybe it thins when there are a lot of births," I added. "What do you think, Michael Ann? Maybe you should have a few more children to keep the Akashic Record in check. We need sun on the crops."

"I think he sounds like an interesting man," said Michael Ann. "What do we know, anyways? I mean, I doubt it's like he says exactly, but there could be something to it." Merry raised an eyebrow. "I know it sounds crazy," she went on. "But I just think there's a lot we don't understand about the world. About the universe."

"Sure," said Merry. She knelt before the baby and put her index finger into his hand, letting his fingers curl around it. "There's plenty we haven't learned yet. But most things can be explained by science. Or they will be eventually." She leaned in and kissed the baby's nose. Michael Ann nodded but said nothing. When she went into the house to nurse, Merry said she must be under the spell of motherhood. "The magic of biology." She sighed and sat down beside me on the swing. "At least I have you," she said. "A fellow scientific mind in this sea of magic."

The following Monday, I found a note on my desk. *Edgar Cayce wants you to pay him a visit. 1321 10th St. After 1 pm.*

I found Edgar asleep his study, head resting on a book. The window was open, and children were fighting in the next yard.

"Edgar," I said. His nose twitched and he opened his eyes, his head still resting on the book. "I'm sorry to wake you, Mr. Cayce."

"Not at all, my man," he said, straightening up and smoothing down his hair. His cheek bore the imprint of the book cover. "I'm glad to see you. I was just having a quick nap. It's how I read, you know."

"What do you mean?"

He said it was something he'd discovered when he was a boy. He'd been a poor student, quite nearly a failure. He was a horrendous speller, and his teacher had visited his father at home to tell him so. Humiliated and angry, his father drilled him for hours, demanding that Edgar spell the week's vocabulary aloud, over and over: *pharmacy, instigate, malfeasance.* But no matter how many times he tried, Edgar could not get it right. He begged reprieve. "A quick nap, and I'll do better." Furious, his father left him alone, and he laid his head on the spelling book and slept. Strangely, when he woke, he knew how to spell every word. He saw them in his mind, the rows of words, the short poems, the grammar lessons. He followed his father around reciting the correct spellings until his father was convinced Edgar had been playing dumb earlier and whipped him anyway. But it had been that way ever since. If he laid his cheek against a book and closed his eyes, he woke with his mind full of the book's contents.

"What were you reading just now?" He held the book out. A book on folk remedies. "It's actually unusual to find a book on such practices," Edgar said. "Most of this knowledge is passed from generation to generation, in kitchens and sickrooms. It's rarely written down and almost never published."

I asked him what he had learned during his nap, and his eyes fluttered a little, the lashes batting. He recited: "For a fever, steep white and black willow leaves to make a tea. For an infection of the skin, a poultice of yarrow and jimson weed will draw it out."

I opened the book, and while I scanned its pages, Edgar continued with a monotonous stream of remedies. Whether he had absorbed the information magically or memorized it at some earlier date, I was impressed.

He invited me to the kitchen for tea. His wife was out. He hoped I wouldn't mind that tea at their house was a casual affair. As I followed him out of the room, I noticed he was barefoot.

Over tea and cookies, he told me more of his story. He had been clairvoyant all his life, he said, although it had taken him years to understand his power, to tap into it at will, to make use of it. As a child, he had been afraid of it, terrified that the devil was speaking through him, but now he was confident the gift came from God.

"Call it what you will," he said. "And it's been called just about everything. Common sense, dumb luck, magic, medicine, probability, placebo effect, playing the odds, rolling the dice, conjuring, lying, fantasy. . . . What it comes down to is that, under certain circumstances, I can read the Akashic Record like the rest of you read the newspaper."

"What does it look like?" I asked. "The Akashic Record?" I imagined it as a glowing haze along the horizon, like the mist over the tobacco fields in July. "Does it have Hebrew letters?"

Edgar professed his conscious mind didn't know any better than me, though he was fairly certain it had nothing to do with Hebrew letters. "Only my soul reads it," he said. "Only the soul can read a language without letters, without sound or voice or breath."

"Why did you want to talk to me?" I asked. "I don't have evidence of your fraud, but there's no way I'm going to promote you."

"I don't know," he said. "Intuition, I suppose." He said he had dreamt of me, and we had held a ball of light between us, balancing it on our fingertips. Now, in waking life, he pushed the plate of cookies toward me, and I took one. The sun had rounded a corner of the house so it was slanting through the kitchen, revealing dust motes, spinning and drifting. Perhaps his dream should have alarmed me, but I felt strangely at ease listening to his mumbo jumbo, sipping tea in that sunlit kitchen. I asked him to tell me more about how he had become a "medical clairvoyant."

Maybe, he said, it had all begun at the age of three, when he fell from a fencepost onto a board. A nail pierced his skin and went straight through his skull. His father pulled him off the nail, washed the wound with turpentine, and bandaged it. The incident was mostly forgotten, but occasionally people wondered about its lasting effects.

And then, for years, when Edgar played in the backyard, building towers and cities of mud, he spoke with people who no one else could see, people from Egypt and Persia. This was Kentucky in the early 1880s: he was four years old, and no one in his family had ever been to Egypt or Persia. How would such a small boy have heard of such places? But Edgar said his friends were from these lands of hard-baked dirt, cut ivory and gold, domes and dates and silk. They wore odd hats, he said, which they wouldn't let him touch, and he understood every word they said.

But things got really strange when his grandfather died. Edgar had loved his grandfather because his grandfather, too, saw the future, and sometimes conversed with people others couldn't see. The second sight, Grandfather called it. Some people said Grandfather's sight was spirits talking, all right, but not the ghostly kind of spirits. Others said the booze was Grandfather's attempt at draining the visions of their power, at muffling that private world of ghosts and voices. After all, Persian men in soft hats and the Civil War soldiers, so recently dead and buried, could terrify a man. They sometimes appeared to Grandfather in blood-soaked uniforms. Maybe booze washed the ghosts to pale watercolor, quieted their moans, or at least brought them down from their horses to look Grandfather in the eye.

But then Grandfather died. He went out on his horse, tipsy from his lunchtime bourbon, and in the middle of the creek his horse stumbled, reared, and threw Grandfather from its back. The horse stepped square in the middle of Grandfather's chest, and Grandfather's head fell back into the river. Someone yelled to Uncle Lou, "Come quick!" But Grandfather's heart had been crushed, along with his femur, and even if his heart had not been stomped upon, he would have drowned long before Uncle Lou pulled him from the river and collapsed on the riverbank, panting and soaked, with Grandfather's body heavy across him.

The aunts laid Grandfather's body out on the table in his Sunday suit and tie, his shoes polished and tied in neat bows. Aunt Cece filled Grandfather's crushed chest with socks and buttoned the shirt over them, then folded his hands over the shirt so you couldn't tell how damaged his body was, how collapsed and empty.

Young Edgar stood on a wooden bench beside the table and studied Grandfather's body. He touched Grandfather's closed eyes. He leaned over the body, listening for breath, then looked up and nodded but not at anyone in particular. He never cried, not even at the graveside when everyone else—the aunts especially, to whom Grandfather had been a harsh and judgmental father—sobbed and twisted their handkerchiefs. But Edgar looked at each mourner's face and nodded, observing their grief.

After the funeral, Edgar took Grandmother's hand. "Why is everyone so sad?" he asked. "Grandfather is okay."

For months after that, Edgar spent afternoons speaking with his dead grandfather in the tobacco barn, which had been their favorite place to converse back when Grandfather was alive. Back then, they would sit on stumps, the long tobacco leaves hanging like mink from the ceiling, growing brittle as they dried. Now that Grandfather was dead, Edgar didn't sit down for their talks but stood in the center of the barn, his head tipped back a little, as if he were looking up at the man. Edgar was only six, so pretty much everyone was taller than him, including the ghost of his grandfather. On days that Edgar did not find Grandfather in the barn, he ran through the barn in loops, in one door, out the other, and back around to the front again, his arms spread like wings.

When Aunt Cece asked Edgar why he spent so much time out in that dark old barn all by hisself, Edgar replied that he wasn't alone. He described how Grandfather puffed on a pipe while they talked.

"What do y'all talk about?" Aunt Cece asked.

"This and that," said Edgar. "Once he showed me how to pack a pipe and which type of tobacco is best for when I have a little extra money."

Cece shrugged. What use did the dead have for tobacco?

"It's the thing he misses about living," Edgar said, though Cece had not spoken her question aloud. "Even though he's always got his pipe in his mouth, he can't get a really satisfying smoke now that he's dead. I think that's why he wants to talk about it. Because he misses it."

Across from me now, Edgar paused and took a swallow of tea. The sun was low, and the shadows fell long across the kitchen.

"Why don't we stop there," he said. "I'm talking your ear off. And we can meet again another day."

"But how did you come to believe your vision was a gift from God?" I asked. "If it were me, I'd worry about my sanity. Other people have heard voices, of course. It's not usually a welcome condition."

Edgar nodded. "It took me a long time to learn," he said. "Like I said earlier, there's nothing special about my conscious mind. But I can tell you how I came to love the Word of God."

"Sure," I said, though God was generally of little interest to me.

"It all started with a stick," he said. At twelve, he tripped on a stick in the woods and it impaled his groin. He lay in bed for months, reading the Bible while the wound festered. Finally, Aunt Cece made a tea of cobwebs and water, a remedy not even recorded in the folk annals, and soon enough, Edgar was up and about again, but by then he'd fallen in love. His mother sewed a new, larger pocket in the back of his overalls so he could carry his Bible with him at all times.

Edgar came around to thinking that particular stick had in fact been God's instrument. If he had not tripped on that stick, he would not have been sick in bed for so long, and then he may not have had time to fall in love with God's Word. But nevertheless, he lost touch with the Little People, and his Grandfather no longer visited with him. He was a teenager, and there were young women to court, jobs to hold down, and he saw little value in talking with the dead when there was a future to be blazed.

"But I've talked enough for today," he said. He looked me in the eyes. "Thank you for listening to me." He extended a hand to help me up and kept my hand for a moment, holding it in both of his. "I'm not in the business of convincing people, Charlie. They either believe me or they don't, and I only help believers. The others don't ask. But I can't help but wonder what would convince you?"

"Nothing," I said. "I'm not in the business of being convinced."

He sighed a little but smiled. He invited me to an event the next evening, a private reading in the home of a local widow. "People always want to know about their past lives," he said. "At the very least, I expect you'll find it entertaining."

◆◆◆

The reading was to take place in a big house on Walnut Street, an easy walk from my office, but I stopped by Merry's first. She hadn't met Edgar, and I thought she'd be amused. Plus, she might help me ferret out his deceit. She came to the door with her hair in curls, but when I told her where I was headed, she refused to join me.

"What are you after, Charlie?" she said. "Didn't you say you had six obituaries to write before Wednesday? It matters, you know. Those people who died—their families want to see them honored."

She had never cared before. Not about the deaths, births, and marriages. That stuff was barely better than the gossip pages.

"You just don't like him," I said.

"Why should I? He's a con man. You've already written about him once. Any more attention is free publicity. You'll be his accomplice."

"He's fairly entertaining," I said. "And I kind of like the man."

She laughed loudly. "That much is obvious. What happened to *Science! Industry!?*" She punched the air in triumph. She shook her head. "He's just another hillbilly. . . . I have work to do anyway. I'll be in the lab until late."

The sitting room was hot and dark, full of well-to-do townsfolk in polished shoes, pin curls and lace, rumpled linen suits. All the men had sweaty, thinning hair plastered across their scalps. The women pushed the muggy air around with paper fans. The drapes were drawn tightly shut. The hostess lit a lamp on the table in front of Edgar, who welcomed us, gesturing broadly around the room, pausing to smile at me. Soon enough, he was leaning back in an armchair, feet up, seemingly asleep, his head falling toward his shoulder like a wilted flower.

The hostess read a question from a sheet of paper. "We have noticed that you speak to us of the body in the third person. Who is it that speaks to us? Who are you?"

Edgar's voice was the same as it had been during the previous event, clear and steady, although he sounded irritated, slightly impatient. "I have told you before," he said. "I have told you and told you. I am Edgar. We are Edgar. We are the body and the soul. I am the entity."

The woman nodded gravely, then looked again at the paper. She spoke slowly. "Sometimes you are wrong. You have given wrong answers about the stock market, for instance, or about the nature of someone's death— Mrs. Bronson, for example, died of pneumonia, not, as you predicted, in a fire. Why should we trust your predictions?"

"My friend," he said. This time, there was no trace of irritation. "The future is flexible. It depends upon your actions. I do not have all the answers. But do not limit yourself to your senses, which are good and worthy and make your life lovely but also blind you to those things you cannot touch or see. There are many things that do not make noise and do not fill your noses with their foul or delicate aromas, but they still exist. You must trust the spirit beyond the powers of the body."

The hostess had more questions—we could see them filling most of a page—but the others interrupted her. They were there to hear about who they had been in their past lives. Wasn't that the purpose of the evening? Wasn't that what we were all here for?

"Well, go ahead and ask him," the hostess said, batting away a fly with her long fingers. "Who will go first?" A pause, and then three or four people volunteered at once. "There's plenty of time for all of you."

She gave up her chair, and one at a time, each person sat beside Edgar and asked him who they been in their past life. Without a pause, Edgar answered each in turn. A Civil War soldier. A child who died young. A landowner. A Puritan, driven from England for his religious beliefs. The woman next to me nudged me with her elbow.

"Don't you want to know?" she whispered. "Aren't you just dying to know?"

I shook my head no. I was Charlie Reilly. I had always and only been Charlie Reilly, the child of Mason and Marietta, one in a long line of Kentucky Reillys. A stubborn journalist. A believer in science, industry, and progress.

But then, somehow, I was standing and moving toward the chair. I found myself sitting in it, leaning toward Edgar, speaking quietly to him. "Who was I, Edgar?" I whispered. "Charles Reilly. Where have I been before?"

A wrinkle moved across his forehead like a dog's hide bothered by flies. "You were a child of pioneers," he said. "In a caravan, rolling across the country. You slept on a pile of rugs in the back of the wagon. But one morning, you alone awoke and stepped from the tent into the dawn. The pink sun fell across the long grasses. You watched bison chewing slowly, not 200 meters away, raising their heads one at a time to look at you, and you felt you were one of them. Within a week of that morning, you were dead of dysentery. You were buried on the prairie. Your name was Ambrose Roundy."

When I told Merry about it, she laughed. "Always a sucker for a story, aren't you Charlie?" I felt myself blush, and although I had seen it all perfectly when he spoke of it, I hadn't professed any sort of belief—not then, not now. Merry leaned back against the wooden swing. We were on Michael Ann's front porch, again, though Michael Ann was inside. Her son was sick with a fever. We were sipping gin rickeys, the glasses sparkling with condensation. Merry closed her eyes and put one hand out in front of her as if she were feeling her way through the dark.

"It's coming clear to me now," she said. "I see a hippopotamus. Wait now—it's a baby hippopotamus bathing in the Nile. But oh! Poor thing! A crocodile is approaching! It's attacking the baby hippo! It's you! You're the baby hippo! You're going down in a bloody mess! Your mother hippo is bellowing and moaning. She's snapping at the croc, but it's too late for you, young hippo." She opened her eyes and fluttered her lashes at me. "How'd I do?"

I tried to laugh. "I don't know, Merry," I said. "It isn't as if I believe him, but he's not as absurd as you're making him out to be. And he doesn't ask anything for his services, which is strange for a con man. What's in it for him?"

"Fame," she said. "Notoriety." And even if he wasn't asking for money, she reasoned, his believers would take care of him. They'd invite him for dinner. They'd give him gifts. She said she'd heard about a stockbroker from New York who had offered to build Edgar his own hospital, if he'd "help" with the broker's investments. "All sorts of people believe him," she said. "Not just old Kentucky grammas. People with power. People with money."

"But he isn't asking them to believe. They just do."

"People want to believe, Charlie. You know that. People want to believe in something bigger than themselves. In fairy tales. In a benevolent god. It explains away the chaos. It makes them feel less afraid."

It was my own argument. A million times I had said that fear was a motivating force. If we recognized that we had only this one lifetime to make any sort of difference in the world—not to store up riches in heaven, but to change things on earth—to cure diseases, to invent technology that made lives easier—if we recognized this, we would work harder. Religion and belief in an afterlife made people lazy and complacent. Believers had it easy, I said. All of their decisions were made by someone else. Their fate and the fate of our world was basically out of their hands. It was up to us nonbelievers to get anything done.

I hadn't said a prayer since I was ten. In high school science classes, I had looked through the microscope and witnessed the miracle of cell division, but why attribute it to God? You tip the substance of one test tube into another and, like magic, you make something new. You slice through the smooth skin of the frog and there are its organs, frog after frog nearly identical in shape and arrangement. Ours is mostly an orderly universe, but if it were divine, wouldn't it be perfect? And if it were perfect, it would be like a machine. And machines, I thought, transcended the clumsiness of consciousness. But none of this explained anything. The reasons for my faith in science were as shoddy as reasons others gave for faith in magic, in ghosts, in God. I loved Merry for her scientific mind. I loved way she pared everything down to reason. But what if she was wrong? What if we were wrong? What if, somehow, Edgar's powers were real?

I swallowed the last of my cocktail. "You want another, Ockham?" I asked, raising my empty glass.

She shook her head no. "Let's take a walk into the sunset," she said.

I was reading in my living room when I was startled by a window-rattling knock. It was Merry, and she was a mess—red faced, tangle haired, out of breath. It was her sister, she said. Michael Ann. Or rather, it was Michael Ann's child, feverish and seizing on the hour. For eight hours, Merry said. Eight seizures. He was three months old. It was unlikely he'd live until morning. "Will you come?"

"What do you want me to do?" It came out wrong—too abrupt, too helpless. I took her hand. "Of course I'll come."

"I just want you there. It's awful," she said. She shook her head, as if to shake out the images. "He foams at the mouth. And Michael Ann—" she began to cry. I smoothed her hair while she pressed her face into my shoulder. "Please," she said, pulling me toward the door. "Let's go."

The doctor said the child would die by morning. Michael Ann was with the baby in the bedroom, and Merry went to her while I sat at the kitchen table with Mr. and Mrs. Miller and Michael Ann's husband, Jim. I said how sorry I was, how sad, but everything sounded false, like I was a terrible actor reciting lines from a play, stiff and robotic. I meant my words, but I had no idea how to express them with compassion. When Merry came back, she said Michael Ann had asked her to call Edgar Cayce.

"You can't be serious," said Jim. "The psychic?"

Merry nodded. "I know. But I don't think there's much to lose by calling him. If it's a comfort to her . . ." Merry was opposed to comfort for its own sake, comfort without action—opiate of the masses and such, though in this case it would be opiate of one.

"I don't know," said Jim. "It's not like her. She hasn't slept in two nights. She's not thinking straight. It seems desperate."

"It *is* desperate, Jim," Merry said. "Your son is dying."

So Jim and I went to fetch Edgar, who came with us immediately, not even bothering to put on his coat. His wife kissed him in the doorway. "God be with you," she said.

The baby was heaving and panting in cycles. His eyes were small, watery slits, as if he could neither open nor close them, and his body was covered with a bright pink rash. Edgar was not a large man, but when he placed his hand on the child's chest, it covered the entire torso. The child had been born a few weeks early and was still birdlike, all elbows and fingernails. For a moment I thought it would be best if he died. To live beyond this night would only prolong his illness and his mother's suffering. I squeezed my eyes shut. I opened them. The thought remained. A swift death would be the best thing.

Edgar moved his hand, resting it gently on the baby's forehead in what may have been meant as a gesture of comfort or may have been some sort of reading tactic, a way of absorbing knowledge through his palms. The child lay limp in the crib, only his chest moving, rapidly with shallow breaths.

"I'll see what I can do," Edgar said.

I followed him to the sitting room and helped him get situated on the sofa while the others stood in the doorway. No one said a word. The room seemed full of creaking floorboards, settling furniture, and bugs flying headlong into the windows. The front door slammed— the doctor leaving. Besides keeping the baby comfortable, he had long since given up on treatment, but he wasn't about to stay around to watch anyone hasten the child's death. I couldn't blame him.

In his trance, Edgar spoke of hot water, a peach-tree-bark poultice, and belladonna tincture. Belladonna, a droopy purple flower, grew everywhere around Bowling

Green. Every schoolkid learned to recognize it and to stay away. There was certain to be some growing at the back edge of the yard, where the lawn blurred into forest, but even a few drops would kill the child. Then again, anyone could see that the boy was nearly dead already, his chest wheezing, his eyes in a stupor that was not sleep. We were all braced for the next seizure or the next—the one that would kill him.

I thought of the headstones that marked infant graves, the ones in the shape of a small white lamb. Often a pair of tiny shoes dangled from those stones, the laces tied together, as if for luck on the journey. How I had scoffed at the gesture, the shoes and stones not belonging to any child I had known. The idea that a dead infant would ever need shoes again was absurd. Michael Ann's son only wore socks anyway, and even those he usually kicked off. His feet always struck me as too pink. They looked boiled. But I always found myself touching them. They were smoother than petals. I loved the way his toes reflexively curled in if I touched the bottom of his foot.

Edgar awoke and sat up, blinking. "Did I say anything helpful?" he asked.

Michael Ann and Jim were arguing near the fireplace, quietly, their heads together. Jim was gesturing emphatically. Michael Ann was weeping. Finally, Jim left the room and Michael Ann came to us.

"Thank you, Mr. Cayce," she said. "We're going to try it. Thank you so much for coming here." She looked at me. "Charlie. You'll help?"

Would Michael Ann regret it? Would she blame us? Would she blame herself? Should I try to talk her out of it? The child would die either way, but that didn't mean I had to help. But I found myself nodding. I would help.

In the backyard, I shimmied up a peach tree and peeled its branches with a pocketknife, dropping long strips of bark into the grass below. I had not climbed a tree in years, and I found I was afraid to jump down when I was done.

I considered staying there, wedging my foot in the crook and waiting. Then I thought to jump aggressively so that I might twist or break an ankle. I would be unable to offer any additional help. But I was instinctively sure on my feet, and the tree was not tall. I jumped and barely stumbled. I brought the bark to Merry, who wouldn't look at me and didn't thank me. She dropped the bark into a soup kettle of water, letting it boil until bitter vapor fogged the windows and burned our throats. She dipped muslin swaddling into the water, wrung it around a long-handled spoon, and let it cool. Mrs. Miller brought it to Michael Ann along with some of the bark, and Michael Ann wrapped the baby tight in the hot cloth, tucking strips of bark between the layers.

Edgar waited in the sitting room, occasionally getting up from the sofa to pace, pausing in the doorway of the room where the child lay. It had been almost an hour since his last seizure.

Merry smoothed Michael Ann's hair back from her face, then went back to the kitchen to make the tincture, leaving her sister with the baby, who seemed suddenly calm and exhausted swaddled in the hot sheets. Michael Ann wrapped a blanket around him and held him against her shoulder.

When Merry came back, Michael Ann sat the child on her lap and Merry squeezed the tincture into his mouth with an eyedropper. He coughed and his skin flushed, but he seemed to be sleeping.

We watched the clock, watched the boy, waiting for his body to clench, but he went on sleeping. At least if he died, it seemed he might do it peacefully.

Michael Ann laid him back in his crib and we all leaned over him, watching him take breath after breath after breath. One at a time, we drifted back to the kitchen where we poured cups of tea and held them tight in our hands, feeling the hot porcelain against our palms. No one spoke. Finally, Merry joined us at the table, but soon she got up again and returned with Edgar, who had remained in the dark sitting room.

"Michael Ann's sleeping," Merry said. "Finally."

It had been three and a half hours since the child's last seizure, but no one spoke this aloud. Finally, Edgar took Merry's hand on one side and Mrs. Miller's on the other. "Why don't we pray?" he said, and I took Merry and Jim's hands in my own.

The child lived. He is four years old now and has not had another seizure since that night. It's possible, of course, that Edgar got lucky, that the seizures would have stopped anyway, that their cessation had nothing to do with peach bark or belladonna, that the tincture was not quite strong enough to kill him, although, sick as he was, it seemed a drop or two would have been plenty. I have thought, once or twice, that maybe Merry never added the belladonna to the vodka, never made the toxic mixture, but if this is so, it remains her secret. The child lived.

If you think the poison in the dropper is medicine, it is no sin to squeeze those drops into the child's mouth, but if you think it's poison, you expect to kill the child. Evil lies in your intention, or in your expectation. Edgar believed in the medicine. So did Michael Ann. I gathered the bark. Merry squeezed the drops into the child's mouth. I watched them fall. I let them. I tell myself I acted out of hope, but the truth is that I thought it was poison, and I went along with it anyway. Either I was wrong or I got lucky, but I did not act on faith. I was willing to let him die. By any system, it is inexcusable.

But the child lived. This past Easter morning I watched him race around the yard, collecting hidden eggs and fighting over them with his cousins—my own children. Twins. He sings in the bath like any child. He lived. And all across the city people heard how Edgar had saved him. The opiate of one grew like a potato, but who am I to deny it? The child lived.

That night in Michael Ann's kitchen, in the lingering, bitter steam, I took Merry and Jim's hands, and I listened to Edgar's voice as he prayed. It sounded like a creek just thawed, although he was not in a trance. It was Edgar speaking, not his spirit, not his unconscious mind, and as he spoke, I began to wonder—for the first time since I was a child—about God. Or at least about the afterlife. If maybe there was one after all. Or if maybe there were many. Maybe I was justifying my passivity. Or maybe I had it completely wrong. Maybe I hadn't even begun to imagine the complexity of our world. Maybe our spirits ebb across time and mingle with trees and insects and soil, merge with language and lungs. Maybe, in these fragile bodies, we haven't even begun.

WE ARE A TEEMING WILDERNESS

*I can tell you the exact date that I began to think of
myself in the first-person plural — as a superorganism,
that is, rather than a plain old individual human
being...[These several hundred microbial species with
whom I share this body] which number around 100
trillion, are living (and dying) right now on the surface
of my skin, on my tongue and deep in the coils of my
intestines.*

—Michael Pollan,
"Some of My Best Friends Are Germs"

*Do I contradict myself?
Very well then I contradict myself,
(I am large, I contain multitudes.)*

—Walt Whitman, "Song of Myself"

We, the superorganism known as "Glenn," often
envision an infographic of ourself in the shape of a
man. This infographic is a veritable stained-glass window
of colors and shapes. We imagine our mouth shape as
red, esophagus yellow, sinuses green, gut purple, and
stomach orange. Our brain is a quiet gray, unless pulled
out for close focus in an infographic of its own. Our
groin is a fecund garden. Under a microscope, our groin
would appear as a jungle, full of tiny monkeys climbing

on wiry trees. The groundcover absolutely crawling with life. Blooming and dying and blooming.

Sometimes we, Glenn, swap cells with other super-organisms. We've exchanged plenty of gypsy microbes with the superorganism that goes by "Sophie." Sophie is a garden, too, of course, a verdant Eden. Her infographic would be more purple than ours—female superorganisms have longer intestines—and her jungle includes a tropical cavern. With Sophie, we cross-fertilize. We diversify our ecosystem. Some of us who are now Glenn used to live in or on Sophie. We traveled in caravans from pink cave to red cave. From freckled arm to eyelash. Some of us have even returned to Sophie after a foray into Glenn, and the heartiest of us have traveled back to Glenn yet again. With Sophie we have open borders.

Once, we, Glenn, took a course of penicillin. We had been invaded by an army of streptococci (yellow, fanged). The penicillin slaughtered most of us, along with the invading army. Our cell walls disintegrated. We were naked and tender, as vulnerable as amphibian eggs nesting in a creek bed as the oil spill rainbows nearer, as the mist of Roundup Ready settles over them like a veil. Countless numbers of us shriveled and died. Dead, we traveled the purple byways of our body. We coursed through the blue tributaries, rested in the dark brown pools. We joined the other carcasses for the exodus. Our tiny bodies lay in drifts. For a time, Glenn was sparsely populated, almost a ghost town. But those of us who remained began to recolonize. We accepted new settlers, begging them off Sophie, off hamburgers, off lettuce and doorknobs. We were homesteaders as we had never been before.

When we, Glenn, feel sad, many of us become wanderers in the weeping. We become sailors, adrift on the Sea of Tears, which only bursts its banks occasionally. Our body contains a rust-colored ocean in the lining around our heart. We live on a crust of salt on the surface of our eyes and in the tunnels of our nose. We rest in the pockets of our skull—we call it The Cave of Montesinos. Sometimes, we get restless. But like Sinbad the sailor, we vow to stay, stay, stay. This time, we will remain. We will drift on our homey, stagnant ponds. But just as we settle in, the tide rises. In a splash, we roll down our cheeks. We encounter exotic foreigners—desert dwellers used to traveling by wind or fingertip. We come to rest on sleeves or tissues. Sometimes, we are licked by the swift, broad tongue of the dog. We travel on that meaty sail until the dog licks the baby, or itself, and then we find new resting places. We set up camp in waving fields of fur or on the smooth, powdery expanses of a chubby thigh. We stake our claim in the hot, dark crevasse of baby's elbow.

But we, Glenn, are also raging xenophobes. In particular, we are nervous about silverware in restaurants. We know that the community in a dishwasher is dense, hostile, and well-fed. Those fierce creatures scoff at detergents, eating gravy and whatnot, eating each other, dividing and dividing and dividing. We know that the hands of the workers are wild gardens, too, overrun with weeds and creepers. We picture their dark rituals, their strong armies, and we quiver.

So when we, Glenn, dine in a restaurant, we bring our own silverware tucked into Sophie's purse, sterilized in boiling water and a splash of iodine, wrapped in starched linen and sealed in a ziplock. Sophie sometimes expresses irritation at this practice, but she puts up with it for the sake of peace. She kisses us and smooths our brow. We love it when she smooths our brow. Some of us take the opportunity to jump ship. Escaping on the tips of her fine fingers, we become Sophie.

We take comfort in each other. We, Glenn, tell ourselves that Glenn used to feel lonely, back when we thought of ourselves as singular, back when we called ourselves "I" and "me." *How foolish*, some of us say, *that loneliness, that oversight*. But some of us protest: we feel criticized.

Well, we were all so quiet back then, we tell us, and those of us in the mouth dance and scoot and shuffle like so many Pop Rocks. Gently, we run our index finger along our arm, gathering a cocktail party in the whorls of our fingertip, and we kiss that fingertip, some of us leaping from lips to finger, others from finger to lips. We, Glenn, are never alone.

TWO BIRDS

Until he was seven, Jack had a matching pair of straight legs and long, pale arms that freckled in the summer. His lungs were tucked unseen within his chest, inflating and deflating, tender as jellyfish. Summer evenings, he and his sister, Jane, chased the mosquito truck. Jack was the fastest runner in the neighborhood—faster than Jane, faster than the older neighborhood boys. If he saw the truck amble through an intersection, followed by its billowing cloud of DDT, he was the first to catch it. He held up his hands and caught the mist. He twirled and felt it dampen his legs. He filled his lungs. Through the cloud, a hand would emerge, and he knew Jane had caught up. Giddy and breathless, Jane would soon stumble to the curb, but Jack would keep running. He felt his heart thud in his chest, in his throat, in his fingertips.

Jane was chubby. Their father called her Puff for years after she'd grown tall and somber. "Puff, be so kind as to bring me a drink?" he'd say, and she'd bring it, but before she set it on the table within his reach, she'd make him call her Jane. She wanted to be president and hung a sign on her door that read, "Bennett for President 1980." She was determined to be the first woman president and the youngest.

"What if someone beats you to it?" their father asked. Their mother snorted. "Fat chance."

Jane offered Jack the position of vice president but then reneged and offered the position to her friend Susan. "Susan has the wholesome looks that appeal to voters," she explained one evening, shoveling peas into her mouth. "What's wrong with Jack's looks?" asked their mom. "He's not wholesome?"

"He looks a little sneaky. Sneaky looks run in our family, if you haven't noticed. It's our eyes—they're too close together. We get that from you, Mom. I need to balance my own sneaky looks with someone more wholesome."

Their father said that was a sound theory but that he hoped Jane was considering more than looks in her campaign. He had high hopes for his children, though he didn't have a lot of time for them. On Saturdays he put his feet up and read from *The Complete Works of William Shakespeare*. Sometimes he called Jack "Puck," but usually it was "Jacky-Jack." He sipped whisky on the rocks. Jack liked the sound of the ice cubes clinking when his father swirled the glass.

When Jack had been born, in August of 1945, his father was in England breaking codes for the army. Nothing could be done about that, and to make the best of things, Jack's dad took a class on Shakespeare at Oxford. Two weeks after Jack was born, his father was free to go home, but he was happy in his little Tudor on a quiet English street. Rosebushes were blooming in the front garden. He loved riding his rickety bike through puddles, books bouncing in the basket. He stayed to finish his course.

He arrived home on Christmas Eve when Jack was four months old. He burst through the front door in a swirl of snow.

"Ho, ho, ho!" he said, and kissed his wife on the lips. "You look as beautiful as ever, Ginny." Jack was asleep on the sofa, and his father touched his nose with his index finger. "There's my boy! This one's gonna be the fastest quarter-miler this country's ever seen." Ginny never forgave her husband for the delay.

◆◆◆

The summer Jack turned seven, his mother sent him and Jane to the park almost every day. It was dreadfully hot, but they were forbidden to use the swimming pool because of polio. They were not, under any circumstances, to use the drinking fountain, which was fine with them because the water in it tasted rusty. Every day as they left the house, their mother gave them a dime to buy shaved ice. She stayed home, pressing and folding tea towels, fixing pot roast for their dinner, basting it and turning it until the juices bubbled. Sometimes she ran errands and wasn't home for hours: grocery shopping, getting a haircut and style, or helping Margaret with a sewing pattern. Margaret was her best friend, and sometimes, after talking about their husbands, they ended up kissing, and then they wouldn't see each other for a while.

"Maybe Mom has a lover," Jane said one day, when she and Jack were walking to the park.

"Doesn't she love Dad?" asked Jack.

"You can love more than one person in life," Jane said. "But you're not really supposed to love them at the same time." Jack nodded. Jane was two years older than him. He wondered if he would know as much as she did when he was nine.

The pool was officially closed starting in July. Jack and Jane looked at it through the fence, and it shimmered like a jewel. They imagined it as the fountain of youth and stalked its perimeter, pretending they were Ponce de Leon. If they could sneak one little sip out from under the noses of the Indians, they'd live forever.

In the evening, when the sun was lower and the trees seemed to ooze blue shadows, the park filled with grown-ups, but during the day, it belonged to the kids. Once in a while a mother would push a pram along the sidewalk. These mothers always looked exhausted and sticky, and a little nervous, as though they thought the kids might attack them and steal the baby from its buggy. Mostly, the mothers stayed home, sipping cold drinks, and the fathers went to work.

At the park, Jane was known for telling fortunes. She wrapped a towel around her head and clipped her mother's pink pearl earrings to her earlobes. Jack was her assistant, which meant he collected fees. They took any form of payment: bubblegum or pennies, petals plucked from the rosebushes that grew behind the snack bar, even an especially sharp thorn. Jane said she was training Jack to see the future, but mostly he watched the ants carrying their heavy loads across the dirt. Sometimes he found a crumb in his pocket and set it out for the ants. He imagined them feasting in an underground banquet hall. There was a microscopic world down there, he was sure.

A boy sat cross-legged across from Jane and she took his hand in hers. She ran her fingertips along the lines of his palm and looked into his eyes until he squirmed. Her voice was low and hypnotic.

"What do you wish to know?"

"Will I get a dog for my birthday?" the boy asked.

"Yes," said Jane. "Probably a spaniel."

"All right!" said the boy, and he ran off to tell his friends.

Another boy asked how he could win a million dollars.

"That isn't the sort of question I can answer," said Jane. "You won't ever win a million dollars." The boy picked a pebble from the dirt and threw it as far as he could.

"Some fortune teller you are. You could have made something up, like you make up everything," he said, and kicked the dirt.

A girl asked if her mother's new baby would be a boy or a girl.

"You'll have a brother," Jane said. She patted the girl's hand. "But don't worry; brothers are okay, except that you have to take care of them." She leaned close to the girl and cupped a hand around her mouth. "I've never had a sister. I couldn't tell you what that's like," she whispered. The girl nodded. Her eyes were wide. She walked off slowly, as if already bearing the weight of her future responsibility.

Another girl sat down. She had a red-and-yellow beach ball tucked beneath her arm, and when she tried to set it down, it kept rolling away. Jane took it from her and set it on the old needlework bag she'd adopted when her mother got a new one. Jack and Jane had seen the girl before. She was often at the park with her twin sister. They were lanky, with shining red hair. They looked a little older than Jane. Jane took her hand, and the girl asked her question.

"Who, of all us kids, will get polio this summer?"

In a flicker, Jane saw herself swabbing a thin, twisted leg. Jane dropped the girl's hand as if she'd been burned.

"I don't know," Jane said.

"Some fortune teller," said the girl. She stood up and walked away, red hair swinging.

"Let's go home," Jane said.

The next day Jack and Jane saw the twins, along with two boys, inside the pool fence.

"Hey!" Jane yelled. "What're you doing? How'd you get in there?"

"What's it look like we're doing? We're going swimming," one of the boys said. Both boys were wearing cut-off jeans with frayed edges, and no tee shirts. They were skinny boys, all elbows and ribs.

"Want to come?" said the other boy. He walked over the fence and looked at Jack and Jane, sizing them up.

"Or are you too busy making up stupid fortunes?" said a twin.

"How did you get in there?" Jane said again.

"We climbed the fence," said the boy. "It's easy."

"You guys are crazy. You could die from swimming in that water." Jane shook her head.

"What're you, chicken?"

Jack didn't think it was chicken, really. It was science: swimming pools were dangerous. That's why it was closed.

The first day they got their television, his mom had turned it on, and on the screen Jack saw a man that had been paralyzed by polio. His mom said that lots of kids had gotten polio from swimming pools. *Cesspools*, his mom said. The man on TV had to live in a silver capsule that looked something like a spaceship.

"An iron lung," his mother said. She turned the television off. She explained that polio could cause your lungs to stop working on their own. The iron lung helped the man breathe. She got up and went to the fireplace and took the bellows from their hook. "It's like this," she said, working the bellows so they blew air at Jack's stomach and his tee shirt fluttered. "Inside the capsule it's like a giant bellows pushing and pulling the air through his lungs." The man couldn't leave the iron lung, she said. He had to lie down all the time.

Jack turned the television back on. "I want to see," he said.

The iron lung had gleaming buckles and screws and round windows along its sides. The man's head stuck out the top like a knob and rested on a pillow. The man was at a football game, and the reporter leaned over his face so they could have a conversation.

"Wow," said the reporter. "Wow-ee. Bet you never thought you'd go to a football game again."

The man laughed loudly, showing his teeth and his tongue. "No sir, I sure didn't."

"You're a miracle of modern science," the reporter said.

The twins were taking off their shorts and tee shirts, dropping them in a heap on the concrete. The meaner one had a pair of goggles, which she stuck over her eyes. Her hair was bunched up in the elastic band, making her head look lumpy.

"How could the pool have germs in it if no one's even been in it since June?" she said. "Germs can't live that long."

Jack and Jane watched as the kids ran across the deck and jumped into the clear, blue water. One of the boys let out a wail as he flew through the air. Their splashes were spangled sunlight. It was so hot standing there. Jack held his breath, his cheeks puffed out. His skin grew tight around his skull, and his lungs burned.

"What're you doing?" Jane said. Jack let the breath explode out of him.

"Pretending I'm swimming," Jack said. "Pretending I'm underwater."

The twin without goggles climbed the ladder to the high dive and stepped off the end, like it was the plank on a pirate ship. She fell through the air, stiff and straight. She barely made a splash.

"They'll get caught," Jane said.

But already the kids were gathering up their things and running for the fence, hunched and dripping. They left wet footprints on the cement before heaving themselves over and collapsing in the grass, laughing and pulling on their sneakers and tee shirts.

One of the boys looked over at Jack and Jane. He clutched his throat and made a strangled noise.

"Arrrrgh! . . . I've got the terrible PO-LIO!" His eyes bulged. He pretended to try to stand and fell over on the girls.

"Cut it out," said one twin, pushing him off.

"Let's go," Jane said, grabbing Jack's hand.

They snuck in the back door. Their mother was humming in the kitchen. It felt to Jack like they were the ones who had climbed the fence and gone swimming. He had an urge to change his clothes, as if they were wet and would give him away. Their mother stopped humming.

"Kids?" she said. "What are you doing back so early?" She had supersonic hearing.

They went into the kitchen. Their mom was wearing an apron, but it didn't look like she'd been cooking. She was spotless—each hair pinned into a smooth heap on her head. Her lips were bright with lipstick.

"Jack doesn't feel good," Jane said. "I think he needs a nap."

Jack did his best to look sick, letting his eyes close a little.

"You're sick, honey?" His mom put the back of her hand to his forehead. "You don't feel feverish."

"My stomach hurts," Jack said.

"Well, nothing a little nap and some chicken soup won't take care of. Go on—go to your room. I'll bring you some soup in a little while."

◆ ◆ ◆

That night, Jack and Jane chased the mosquito truck for three blocks before they both stumbled to the curb. The truck drove on. Kids ran out of their houses and chased it down the block. Jack was gasping. They watched the streetlight flicker, and the insects came out and circled beneath it. Jane carried Jack home piggyback because he was too tired to walk.

Jack's nose dripped onto his corn flakes. Jane went to the park, but Jack stayed home and slept. His mother brought him lemon tea with honey. His legs ached. He dreamt of a bird's nest containing two eggs, their milky shells quivering. A yellow beak poked out of one, followed by a chick unfolding its damp feathers. From the other came a wingless chick, raw and naked. Its heart fluttered beneath thin skin. Its mouth opened endlessly until its body crumpled. The healthy chick pecked at it until its little heart ceased thrumming. Then the healthy chick tore bits of gooey flesh from its dead sibling and swallowed them. It stretched its wings. Jack woke, but the thrumming continued in his head. He pushed himself up onto his elbows and found he couldn't get out of bed. He called his mom.

His dad carried him out to the car and the entire family got in. They drove to the hospital and his dad carried him inside. Jane was ordered to stay in the car. After Jack's dad talked to a nurse and his mom wrote on a clipboard, his mother kissed him on the top of his head. Then she dabbed her lips with her handkerchief.

"They won't let us stay, sweetie," she said. Jack's father pulled her away.

"We'll see you soon, Jacky-Jack." His father's voice sounded funny—like a voice coming through a radio speaker. "Be good, now."

Jack was one child in a room full of children, each resting on a narrow cot. Two nurses in peaked caps meandered between the rows but were often gone. The children looked like snowdrifts, sleeping and sniffling. Two boys in a corner passed toy cars back and forth. Jack cried, and the girl on the cot next to him propped herself up on her elbows.

"Are you scared?" she said.

Jack said his legs hurt, but in his mind he saw his mom and dad getting back into the red Fleetline and slamming the doors. His father turned the key and the engine spluttered and they drove off. They stopped for ice cream, and Jane ordered strawberry on a sugar cone. Jane always ordered strawberry. Then they got back in the car and drove and drove, licking their ice cream cones.

The girl on the cot next to Jack's had frayed blonde braids. Clinging to the end of one was a blue ribbon, tied in a lopsided bow. She gave Jack one of her two teddy bears.

"To help you sleep," she said.

Jack was supposed to start second grade. His mother had bought him a package of black socks, two white button-down shirts, and two pairs of navy pants. They were on his bed at home, neatly folded. If he concentrated, he could see them stacked and creased, waiting for him. If he died, he thought, Jane would take the shirts and socks, even though the sleeves would be too short for her. She would roll them up and push them to her elbows.

"What did you do to get sick? I let our cat out of the house and it got hit by a car," the blonde girl said. "That's why I got sick. Because I didn't take good care of God's small creatures that can't take care of themselves. What did you do?"

"What do you mean?" Jack asked.

"What did you do that chapped God's hide? It must have been something bad."

Jack thought. He saw himself and Jane, fingers twisted through the chain link fence around the swimming pool, watching the kids jump in. He saw himself sweeping a dust pile under the rug, saw himself taking a dime off his father's desk, saw himself sitting in the backseat of the Fleetline, jabbing his sister hard between the ribs. He saw himself doing a crazy dance around the living room, singing a war cry at the top of his lungs until his mother, who had been sitting on the couch, reading a magazine, pressed her hands over her ears.

"You kids are making me crazy!" she yelled and left the room.

Then there was that day in the garage. He was rooting through his father's tools, just to see what was there, and he found a packet of cigarettes and a book of matches. He lit the matches, one by one, and watched them burn until he felt their heat near his fingertips. And once, he had thrown a bottle into the gutter just because he wanted to hear it break. He left the shattered pieces there. Maybe a kid or an old lady had cut her foot on them. And once, he had put on his mother's lipstick, and then when his mother found the stained tissues he'd used to wipe it off, he blamed it on Jane.

"You expect me to believe Jack used my lipstick?" his mother said when Jane denied it. "You should be ashamed of yourself, young lady. Stealing *and* lying."

Jane had to wash the dishes three nights in a row. When Jack got into bed the third night, the sheets were wet, and his secret candy stash was missing from under his bed, but he hadn't even tried to get it back. Jane hadn't spoken to him for a week.

"I don't know," Jack said. "I guess I've done a lot of bad things."

"My mom said that it might be good to get sick—that I might get to go to heaven if I die, even though I was bad. She said it's kind of like going to jail. You pay off your debt."

Jack didn't think any of the bad things he had done were bad enough for jail.

That night a nurse came for the blonde girl. She helped the girl up from her cot.

"Say goodbye," the nurse said. "We've got to get you cleaned up. You're going home." The girl bounced up and down on her bed, and the railing fell to the floor with a clatter. "Shh," said the nurse. "Say goodbye quietly now."

The girl forgot her teddy bear. It lay on the floor, partway under her bed, facedown.

"God?" Jack said, very quietly. It was dark in the ward. Even the nurses seemed to have disappeared, but he could hear kids sniffling and wheezing. He pressed his hands together like the statues of saints at church. He tried to think of a way to explain himself, but there didn't seem to be any way out of it. When he'd burned those matches, he'd known he wasn't supposed to. Each time the heat neared his fingertips, he'd feared dropping the match. The flames would leap to the curtains, which would explode in ragged flame; the windows would burst. He had imagined himself running out to the street, screaming and waving his hands, while flames poured out from the broken windows, and firetrucks careened around the corner to his house. All the neighbors would come out to watch. And the day he drove his mom crazy by shouting, he'd seen her look up, her eyes bright and frenzied, but it had been so fun dancing around the living room, and Jane's war whoops only made him want to shout louder.

"God?" Jack said again. "I know it probably doesn't matter now, but I just wanted to say that I'm sorry." He closed his eyes and waited for sleep.

All night the nurses moved like ghosts. Jack's toes stuck up at the end of the bed like twin meringues. Tiny flames licked his eyelids when he closed his eyes. He couldn't get up to use the bathroom, and besides, it wasn't allowed.

"I have to go to the bathroom," he whispered. "God? I have to go to the bathroom." He pulled himself up, grasping the rails of his bed, but soon fell back.

In the morning, he found he had soiled the sheets. He scooted to one side. The nurses never stopped; they were like seagulls circling. Jack lifted a corner of his sheet and saw a brown smear. At lunchtime, he refused to eat. A nurse took him to the toilet, and while he was gone, they took the sheets away.

When he got back to his bed they wrapped him in a sour, wet blanket. It was warm but smelled awful.

"Shhh . . ." said a nurse with black eyes. "Shhh, now. This is good for you."

He was a caterpillar in a cocoon. The cocoon was too tight, its threads pulling ever more snugly around him. The cocoon began to spin, hotter and whiter. Maybe this was hell, and hell was inside the sun, and there were a million children dancing around his cocoon in a circle, holding hands, but he couldn't see them. It was too bright. They were sickly, twisted silhouettes. Their heads were too small. And they were completely silent. The cocoon tightened.

Ginny was on the telephone, her mouth moving like a fish's. She twirled the cord. She pulled a pin from her hair and studied it. Jane opened the refrigerator and stuck her index finger into a bowl of whipped cream, then popped her finger into her mouth. Ginny smacked Jane's hand, which was still in her mouth.

"Ow," Jane said.

"Margaret, I have to go," Ginny said into the phone. She hung up. "Go wash your hands," she said to Jane. Jane left the room, but instead of hearing the water run in the bathroom, Ginny heard the back door slam.

Margaret was Ginny's biggest secret, and what good would it do to confess? Those little kisses, they were scraps in the scope of a life. They were slivers. The first time it happened, almost a year ago, they had been talking for hours about their mothers, and about the Japanese, and about their school days, now long past. She and Margaret had each seen one ghost in their lives: she of her grandmother, and Margaret of an unknown man with the most beautiful, pale hands. They both had thought, when they were girls, that love would be different from the way it turned out. They agreed—love was quieter than expected. It seemed they could go on talking to each other forever.

That afternoon, when they first kissed, her children were far away, in a dream of their own—her sweet, grubby chickens. Her husband was probably sitting around a table with a bunch of other men, their beards growing ever so slowly, roughing up their skin. They were probably smoking cigars, laughing their deep, rolling laughs. But she was sitting next to Margaret in the safe, soft light of Margaret's living room. The world outside was full of soft green fields that stretched from Margaret's front door to California, across Japan, across the Sahara. When Margaret leaned toward her, it had seemed the most logical thing in the world. Why shouldn't they kiss each other? But afterward, the green fields vanished. The light in Margaret's living room was too bright. There were tiny blue veins around Margaret's eyes, and the skin around her nose was flaking. Ginny got up from the sofa and tripped over a wrinkle in the rug. Margaret's hands steadied her.

"Ginny," Margaret said. "Don't do this."

"It's fine," she said. "I'm fine. Aren't you fine? It's fine. I'm going to go home now. I'm late starting dinner."

They had kissed four times since then, and every time it had ended similarly—but those moments beforehand! She kept falling into the same trap. And now Jack had polio.

"Oh, Jacky," she sighed. "I'm so sorry."

Jane didn't wash her hands but went to the backyard. The grass was getting long and yellow. Their dad had forgotten to water it, and he certainly hadn't mowed lately. In one corner of the yard there was a sandbox. Jane and Jack never played in it anymore, and a toy dump truck lay on its side, half buried. Jane pulled it out and set it in the grass. She stood in the middle of the sandbox with a long stick, closed her eyes, and turned in a circle, dragging the stick, enclosing herself in a circle.

"Keep me safe and keep me sealed," she said. "Keep me safe and keep me sealed. Keep me safe and keep me sealed." She knelt in the circle. "JackJackJackJackJack," she said. "Be okay." She dusted the sand off her hands.

Jack had a comic book that starred a silver robot, a willowy spaceman in a round helmet, and a boy with a gun that shot purple flames. He flipped through the book over and over. He marked off the days on the back with a pencil. He drew the third mark with a shaky hand.

A nurse fed him because he couldn't hold the spoon. Soup dribbled down his chin and she scraped it up without speaking. When she put the spoon to his mouth, her eyes followed. When he slurped, she looked away. When she looked at him, her eyes were like a cave he could enter, a place where it would be cool and dark, but when she looked away, they were only eyes. She did not touch him. The soup traveled a great distance on its way to Jack's mouth, most of it dripping on the bib she had tied around his neck.

Jane promised not to pretend to know the future when she didn't. Had she stepped on God's toes? "Sorry, God. Sorry, sorry," she said, doing the sign of the cross for good measure. "Sorry, God and Jesus."

Ginny promised to be faithful to her husband in thought and in deed. She talked to Margaret on the phone, but when Margaret stopped by with a casserole, she didn't look at Margaret's slim waist. Yes, Margaret's hair was gleaming in the sun, but so what? "Thank you," Ginny said, accepting the warm dish. "You're such a good friend." They talked for a moment, Margaret standing on the front steps, Ginny holding the door open with her hip, the casserole dish warm against her arms, but Ginny did not invite Margaret in.

Jack's dad promised to stop reading Yeats at work. He shoved the pocket volume to the back of the bottom drawer of his desk. When he got home, he kissed his wife. He said, "How are you?" He said, "How are my children?" He waited for her answers.

In the dark, Jack listened to the other children snore. He tried to see the nurses in the doorway but could barely turn his head. His lungs were sticky and he couldn't cough. A nurse leaned over him and called another, who came quickly with a wheelchair. They wheeled Jack into the bright hallway and then into a room full of gleaming metal machines—the iron lung room. There must have been a dozen of them, buckled and shining in the shadows. Jack's head was full of a sound like ocean waves, but over the din he heard the machines wheezing. There was an empty one for Jack, and the nurses unhinged it. They lifted him from his wheelchair and slid him into the lung. A white rubber ring sealed around his neck. A mirror was positioned above his face and the nurses tilted it so Jack could see what was going on behind him. They were talking—he could tell because their mouths were moving—but he couldn't make out a word.

He slept, listening to the bellows whoosh and wheeze. In his dreams, a fire flickered and flared.

Sunlight glared off the mirror. Even with his eyes closed, Jack could see the brightness on his eyelids. He opened his eyes. His favorite nurse was there. How long had he been sleeping? The nurse took a comb from her pocket and ran it through his hair. He studied the weave of her cotton uniform in the mirror. Her hand moved over his face, gripping the plastic comb loosely, preparing for another stroke.

"You're a lucky one," she said. "You're going to be all right."

Jack could only speak on the exhales. His words were a breath infused with sound.

"Will I go to football games like this?" he asked.

"You're not strong enough to breathe on your own now, but you might get stronger. We have to wait and see."

"Will I have to live in here?"

"I just don't know, sweetie," she said. She leaned over him. Her skin was smooth as clay. She pressed a cool hand to his cheek, and she straightened up and took her hand away. In the mirror, he watched her walk on to the next patient.

A doctor came and opened the lung. He slid Jack's body out so Jack could see it: his arms, his stomach, his legs and feet, his chest rising and falling.

"I'm breathing," Jack said.

"You are, but your lungs are weak. You won't be able to breathe out here for long, but I think you can handle a few minutes. It's time to see how you're doing." He folded the sheet to Jack's waist and lifted a foot. Jack saw that his leg was incredibly thin—a bone covered with pale, loose skin.

"My leg is melted," Jack said.

"Yes, your legs are very thin. You haven't been able to use your muscles, so they've gotten small. Can you push on my hand?" the doctor said. He waited. Silently, Jack told his leg to push, but it didn't seem to be listening. Finally, the doctor said, "Good," and switched legs. Jack breathed for ten minutes before the doctor slid him back into the lung and buckled it around him.

Jane was not allowed in the ward, but their parents went to visit Jack. In the car they agreed that optimism was best. Jack's father waved in the mirror at Jack as he approached.

"Jacky-Jack, how are ya?" He slapped the side of the lung and Jack's lungs stuttered mid-wheeze.

"Hi," Jack said.

"You're looking fine, my boy. As well as can be expected."

His mother's eyes glistened.

"Jacky," she said. She pushed his hair from his forehead. "My Jacky."

"Ginny," Jack's dad warned.

"Do I get to go home?" Jack asked. "Are you here to take me home?"

"Not yet. Not just yet," said his father. "Are you feeling better?"

On the exhale, Jack said yes.

"They say the worst is past."

"It's your birthday tomorrow," his mother said. "Seven years old. You've got a long life ahead of you. You're a survivor now, Jack."

She settled in a chair beside Jack's head and opened an illustrated copy of *Alice in Wonderland*. In the mirror,

Jack watched the doctors and nurses coming and going. He listened to their shoes squeak across the floor. He listened to the lung, endlessly wheezing, pushing the air in and out of his body.

It was August and the dandelions had gone to seed. Jane stood on the new sidewalk at the edge of a vacant lot, full of pale, seeded globes. The wind scattered some of the seeds, leaving bare stalks, and Jane ran into the lot after the seeds, her hands raised, until she tripped. In the grass was a spine, picked clean and white, curved like a snake. It was thin and long—a cat's probably. The world swarmed with danger.

"Leave it alone." Jane said aloud to herself. "You are going to be president. *President*." But then she knelt and lifted the spine anyway. It swung from her hands like a brittle rope. She stood, cradling it like a baby.

a Hotel Patio
in Orizaba. 8

A HOTEL PATIO IN ORIZABA

A town at the base of a volcano. A town where the land was flattened by rivers and lava and mud. A town where wrinkled men loiter between cobblestone streets and pink stucco buildings, one foot against the wall, the other against the earth. Like storks, they stand smoking fat cigars in the shade of their wide-brimmed hats, and their eyes follow a pair of trim legs on their way around the corner. A hotel patio where tourists sit with their *tazas de café*, dark and sweet, and pastries with cinnamon and sugar, and slices of pineapple on small white plates. The fountain is dry; it's been years since it flowed. The basin, full of dried leaves, is painted Holy-Mary-Mother-of-God blue, but the plaster is cracked, the pipes and fittings verdigrised and lime-crusted. High above, leaves and vines hang like Rapunzel's hair, falling over the wall into the courtyard. On the balcony, a man, an American, leans on his elbows, mindlessly watching the people below, their newspapers catching the sun, while behind him, through the open French doors, through the dark room with the unmade bed and rumpled pillows, in the bathroom with the cold white tiles, a woman vomits into the toilet, keeping her hair out of it this time by tucking it into her collar. And inside the woman, a cluster of cells has been dividing for nine precarious weeks—no knowing yet if they'll continue. She wipes her mouth with the back of her hand and tries to be grateful for the sickness. *All of this is part of it,* she tells herself. *Hold still and listen.* And for a moment, even the plants cease their creeping. *Hold still,* she says again, listening for the cells. *Zygote,* she whispers. *Little Goat.* But she has been here before, listening, and that time the cells remained just that, and then they broke apart and left her and became nothing again. She is trying not to get attached. A bird flies across the sky above the courtyard, singing. It pulls its fleeting shadow across the stones below and is gone.

ANATOMY OF
THE EYE

Dr. Ignatz von Peczely is convinced: The eye is a map of the body. Each organ, each muscle, each bone correlates with a region of the iris. When a tumor grows in the stomach, the iris reflects it as an inky blot at the center. When the spleen swells with infection, a cloudy stripe manifests in the lower left quadrant. Each body part has its place in the eye, and by studying this map, Ignatz can detect illness. The scalpel lies cold upon its table; he nips the problem with herbs. And if herbs are not enough, at least the surgeon will know where to begin. He can slice with precision.

The patient: Mara Vargha. Eighteen years old, complaining of lower abdominal pain. Her skin is pale. Her hair black and tangled. Her nose so slightly crooked. The doctor has looked at so many eyes, he rarely notices beauty, but Mara's night-sky eyes give him pause. At first glance they appear densely fibered, but when she turns toward the lantern and her iris catches light, they bloom infinitely inward.

She picks anxiously at the cuticles of her left hand with the ragged fingernails of her right.

"Vargha," he says. "You're the daughter of the shopkeeper? On Vaci Street?"

She nods, keeps picking.

"Best kolbasz in town," he says.

Miklós Vargha, Mara's father, is known for his cold demeanor. Her mother, Ignatz knows, has been dead for years. It is said she died of heartbreak because her husband was so loveless, but others say it was her death that soured him. Either way, Mara's father is the sort of man you don't greet unless you're looking for a glare.

"You're his only child?" Ignatz asks.

"There's also Anna. She's six. My father remarried."

Her voice conjures spring leaves unfurling. He draws a little leaf in the margin of his notes.

"Well," he says, "let's have a look." He considers the garlicky soup he ate for lunch and catches his breath as he leans in and examines her eyes.

"Densely woven fibers—you have a strong constitution—but it looks like your lymphatic system is weak. Is your skin always dry?"

She runs the back of her hand along the length of her arm, and fine flakes of dead skin scatter.

"Dry skin is nothing," she says. "I rub it with oil when it's itchy. But these stomach pains—sometimes I double over just to stay standing. Last Tuesday I couldn't even get out of bed."

He leans closer. A cyst? The innermost blue of her iris, the region that reflects the stomach, is smooth and flawless. But in the lower third, at four o'clock, there is a slight braiding, a pair of pale haloes—a sign of anxiousness.

"Have you been nervous about something? Worrying?"

"I was born nervous," she says, smiling.

Ignatz wants to touch her lips, her eyelids. He takes a brown vial from the shelf behind her and holds it up between them.

"Calcarea carbonica," he says. "It comes from oyster shells. Three drops in small glass of water three times a day should help. You could try ginger tea, too, to soothe your stomach. If you're still having pain in a week, come see me again."

He presses the vial into her palm and folds her fingers around it. She stands and thanks him.

"And Miss Vargha—"

"Yes?"

"Try to relax. Go to the baths. Soak. Breathe deeply. Stretch your limbs."

"Thank you." She closes the door behind her when she leaves.

In the mirror, Ignatz studies his own eyes. His pupils are dilated, gaping.

On a tiny funnel of a street of dusty shops, Ignatz has purchased packets of pocket-sized drawings: women with open bodices, their dresses rumpled around their waists, breasts and shoulders bared. He studies these drawings at his kitchen table and in his armchair. Before sleep he lies in bed and flips through his collection. The corners are bent, the images smudged.

His anatomy professor owned a wax anatomical model, a female with long brown hair and glossy lips, imported from Florence. During his third year of school, after Ignatz had proven himself a serious and innovative student, his professor allowed him access to the room where the model reclined, with the promise he'd wear gloves when touching her and handle her with utmost care. Ignatz spent hours in that darkened room, where the walls were draped with navy velvet and the figure lay on a cushion of white satin. The model's eyes were open, though glazed. Her hands lay gracefully at her sides; her long, dark hair was spread around her face and over her shoulders. Her breasts were full and round, her nipples erect. Through her wax skin a network of bluish veins was visible. One leg lay straight and flat upon the platform, the other was bent slightly, at the knee, turned outward. The entire façade of her torso could be removed in pieces—breasts, ribcage, lungs. He could view her glossy heart, her entrails neatly coiled. These organs, too, lifted and revealed her empty stomach, and a tiny fetus, almost fully developed, curled in her womb.

And once, when his mother was still alive, Ignatz went with a friend to a country house where a man could hire a woman for sex. His friend gulped brandy and led his chosen woman out of the dim parlor. Sober, Ignatz chose the youngest-looking of the three remaining women. Her cheeks were round and pink.

"I don't want anything but to look," he said. "I want to study you, for medicine, and draw some pictures."

"No drawings," she said. "My father thinks I'm a barmaid. You'd break his heart."

"No one will see them. They're for me alone—for medicine."

She didn't believe him. She pulled him in and placed his hands on her hips, pressed her body into his. She smelled vaguely of roasted meat, vaguely of lavender. She nuzzled his neck with her cheek and he forgot about the drawings. It was all over in a matter of minutes.

When Ignatz got home, he was sure his mother knew where he had been. He couldn't look at her.

"Are you sick?" she asked, placing a hand against his cheek. He mumbled and pushed past her. He splashed his face with water and shut himself in his father's old office, determined to study, but he could not concentrate. His hands still felt the woman's flesh, but in his mind her face was that of the wax model. He squeezed his hands into fists, but the gesture was useless. Her flesh lingered, soft and fat.

Ignatz understands the machinations of his body. He is an animal, like any animal, and sex is his natural impulse, but unlike his dog, who begs for affection and table scraps, unlike the deer that invade the garden at dusk, he has control over such impulses. He has a brain; he has a choice in the matter.

Ignatz has tested his hypothesis by swinging his left arm in circles, exhausting his shoulder joint, then rushing to check his eyes in the mirror. Is that a pale spot in the upper quadrant? He rubbed his skin with fine-grained sandpaper—a patch on his neck, a patch on his thigh. If there was a change, it was in the outermost ring of his iris, which made sense, he thought—the rim was the skin of the iris, containing it as skin contains blood, muscle, and bone. He once wrapped his head in a blanket and screamed, trying to tear his vocal cords, but even after his voice grew hoarse, he could not see evidence of it in his iris. But he has faith—his patients' eyes have taught him a great deal.

On the wall of his office he has a chart, the cumulative map of his discoveries. A baby with croup has a dark ring in the center of her iris. Asthmatics and pneumonia patients often share the dark ring with the croupy baby. He's written *lungs* in a ring around the pupil.

A woman with a sluggish thyroid has a white half-moon lodged at nine o'clock in both eyes, something like a fingernail clipping. He's seen the half-moon in three other thyroid patients, not to mention their eyes were bulging and overripe. On his chart he penciled the word *thyroid* in the nine-o'clock region. Brown-eyed patients tend toward circulatory problems, malfunctioning livers, and low energy. Blue eyes suffer weak lymphatic systems—fluids flow when they shouldn't and dry up when they should flow. They contract tonsillitis more often, suffer asthma and sinus problems. Their scalps are flaky. They complain of itchy skin, mysterious oozings and swellings. Green eyes suffer the whole array.

Soon, he hopes to diagnose the illness before the patient even speaks.

Ignatz goes to the public baths on Tuesdays and Saturdays, but he's never seen Mara Vargha there. He'd certainly remember if he had. He tries Wednesday, but she isn't there. On Thursday, he shuffles his papers into a pile, planning to work at home after the baths. Again, she is not there.

Saturday, he bathes earlier than usual. He lingers, gliding across the surface like a water bug. He stands beneath a carved marble head, its mouth a spitting O, and steamy water spills over his face. Perhaps Mara goes to the other bathhouse.

He's gathering his sandals from the edge of the pool when, suddenly, she is there, an apparition from the steam. She is wrapped in a white silk robe, her skin even paler than he remembers it. He cannot see her eyes through the mist, but he knows it is her.

"Doctor," she says.

He opens his mouth to tell her he is glad to see she is obeying his orders, but no sound escapes. The steam thins and they stand in clear, dry air, blinking.

"Relaxing?" he says, finally.

"Yes. I'm with my sister."

Ignatz coughs, then manages to ask Mara if she's feeling any better. Before she answers, a little girl approaches and takes her hand. "Come on," the girl says, tugging. "It's cold."

"You go," Mara says. "I'll catch up."

"Your sister's very small," Ignatz says, as the girl runs toward the changing room.

"She's the tallest in her class," Mara says.

"Oh." Ignatz smooths his thinning hair. It is the wispy hair of a young child and there is little left of it. Mara studies him, her face slack. She begins to speak but then shakes her head and closes her eyes, as if to start over. For a moment, he sees her as she would look sleeping, imagines a room full of light and open windows. What a child she must have been—alone with her stern father, choosing her own dresses, combing her wild hair, playing alone in some corner of her father's store.

"I've got to go," she says.

Ignatz's father, a lawyer, worried himself into the grave when Ignatz was still a boy. Ignatz remembers his father's eyeglasses slipping endlessly down his nose, the many mornings he found his father asleep in his study, a book facedown on his chest. It was Ignatz's mother who raised him, sent him to school with a coin tucked in his mitten so he could buy a sweet on the way home. It was his mother who mended his clothing, even taught him to chop wood.

"Do you love me?" she asked each night, tucking him into bed, years after tucking in became unnecessary. "Tell me you love me."

"I love you, Mother," he would say.

"I know. I know you do. And I love you."

Boys, his mother said, were inclined toward disorder. She once caught him throwing crabapples at a girl who was carrying a stack of folded linens past their house.

"I suppose you couldn't help it," his mother said, grabbing his arm a little too tightly. "All that clean cloth." She took everything from his room then, his collection of burrs, his books and games, the portrait of his father that hung on the wall. Ignatz slept with bare walls, bare shelves, white sheets.

Now, on the table beside his bed, he keeps a book and a glass of water.

His mother died three years ago, when he was twenty-two and still in medical school. Her death came quickly. One evening she complained of pain in her lower back, and Ignatz rubbed it for her. He propped her feet upon a pillow, had her lean against a steamy towel. If he had known how bad it was, he would have taken her to the surgeon, had him look beneath her skin. In a matter of days, the whites of her eyes were yellow. He fed her milk thistle tea. She sat in the garden, watching birds feed, but her decline was irrevocable.

Ignatz stood beside her grave with only a handful of people. With each shovelful of dirt, he thought of all he did not yet understand.

The diagram: two black circles for the pupils. Around this Ignatz has drawn spokes and rings. A tiny spot is devoted to the gallbladder. Another to the heart. At the top of the iris, pie-shaped slices are devoted to the higher body parts—brain, ear, mastoid. Middle slices coincide with middle parts—esophagus, kidney, pelvis. Bottom slices with bottom parts—thighs, ankles, metatarsals.

The brain is reflected at the top and center. It's a large section, considering the size ratio of brain to body, but the brain is an important site. It is divided in two: half devoted to physical function, half to emotional. The dividing line reflects the animate life source—something like the soul. When a creature suffers melancholy or despair, this band grows cloudy. When a creature is dying, the band grows opaque. If a creature is in love, will it glimmer? Will it glow?

Mara returns for a second consultation. He checks both eyes and finds that the nerve rings have intensified, like ripples in a pool, but there is no glowing band.

"The medicine hasn't helped?"

"The pain is worse," she says. "I couldn't even leave the house yesterday. And almost every morning, I get sick."

"Is it an ache? A stab?"

"Both. It throbs. Here," she says, pointing to a spot above her right hip. "It stabs here, but I feel it all down my leg. I feel it in my elbow sometimes."

"You've really got to relax. See?" Ignatz holds the mirror for her. "Those rings—those are nerve rings."

"Pain makes me tense."

He touches her temple with his index finger. She is steady. He sees his reflection in her pupils, a tiny toy man.

In his early days of looking at eyes, Ignatz was continually amazed that the pupil seemed a gateway to infinite space. He knew it was a small darkness, leading only to the back of the eye—a brief tunnel for light and image. Looking into Mara's eyes, he remembers that sensation of infinity. With his thumb and index knuckle her turns her face toward the light. It is the same gesture he would use if he were about to kiss her. She is pliant, her head smoothly turning. There is no lesion in the ovarian region of her iris.

"Lean back," he says. He guides her body back in the chair. He could have her unbutton her dress to give him closer access to her organs. He should, but he can't. His hands are shaking. He presses her abdomen with his index and middle finger, feeling for peculiarities, watching her face for pain. Her lips are a tight line.

"Does this hurt?"

"Not particularly," she says.

"Raspberries," he says, standing straight. "They'll increase your womanly secretions. Eat them at every meal. Maybe that will help."

"Maybe?"

"I know that isn't what you want to hear, but it's how these things work. We try one thing. We try another."

"What if there isn't time for all this trying?"

"Mara," Ignatz says. "Miss Vargha. The body is mysterious and complicated. I'm trying to help."

She folds her hands over her stomach and looks away.

"I don't know what to tell you," he says.

"Are there things the eyes don't reveal?" she asks.

"They show most things."

"But not everything."

"The body is—"

"Yes, yes. Mysterious and complicated."

When she leaves, Ignatz watches her out the window. She crosses the street as if sliding on ice. Her shoulders are square, head level. His nervousness, his distraction—unprofessional, he knows. There is no lilt in her step.

Ignatz was not a star pupil in medical school. His breakthrough came the day he volunteered his services to a group of political prisoners—students and bearded radicals who were captured when they stormed the Buda fortress. They wanted a new constitution, equal taxes for all, free press, land rights for peasants. There was no end to it.

The prisoners wanted to tell Ignatz their stories. How they'd been shoved and jostled. How they'd fallen on the steps and been trampled. The tumult of limbs. The grabbing hands. The hyper-extended knees and open mouths.

He was examining a man with a broken left leg when he made his discovery. White sunlight fell across the prisoner's collarbone, leaving his body in shadow but illuminating his eyes, which were pale blue. He was scruffy and musty-smelling, and he made Ignatz nervous. In his left eye there was a black line, stark against the pallor of his wintry irises. It extended straight from his pupil to the edge, like a crack on the surface of a frozen lake.

"It's my leg you should be looking at," the man said. "My leg's broken."

But his eye held the secret. Ignatz had seen such a line before.

He was eleven that time. Through luck or fate he captured an owl on a winter morning. He wrestled it in the snow and managed to wrap it in his coat. They lay together, boy and owl, until he felt the kicking subside, but in the struggle, he had broken its leg.

Ignatz settled the owl in the barn. Gray light filtered through the open door, and the air came to life with floating bits of straw, dust, and feathers. He fixed the handle of a broom to the side of an empty stall as a perch. He fed the owl twice a day: scraps of jerky from the pantry, lesser bits of horse and goat he purchased from the butcher for pennies. He set traps to catch the scurrying mice the owl could not catch for herself. He was careful not to get too close, setting the food where she could reach. Day after day she fixed him in her yellow gaze—monochromatic but for an inky stripe running vertically through the lower half of her eye, pooling at the bottom. She never ate in his presence.

In the house Ignatz found his mother's silver mirror. He perched at the end of his bed and turned toward the frosty window to study his own eyes. They were brown with a reddish ring at the center. He found a black speck in the right eye, like a freckle on two mingled tones of brown. He had once helped his mother bake a cake with two types of chocolate, which they melted on the stove. Ignatz swirled them together with a wooden spoon. His eyes looked like that.

The owl's leg healed surprisingly straight. Her eyes, too, were changed. In place of the black line was a thin, white line, like a filigree of bone. On a warm, clear day he released her. She flew from the barn on tremendous, silent wings, and Ignatz stood alone.

Ignatz splinted the prisoner's leg. He returned three times to watch the man's eyes for change. The black line didn't turn white, as it had in the owl's eye, but it seemed to grow thinner, more threadlike.

Ignatz walks his dog, Grimaszka, along Vaci Street. Grimaszka is a Puli, a swishing black mop. Ignatz jokes that he only knows which end is her face by her tongue, which is always hanging, lolling and pink. As he nears Mara's father's shop, he sees her stepping outside with a tall man. She and the man have their heads inclined toward each other. She steps over a blowing bit of paper. She laughs at something the man has said, and her curls shake. The man is incredibly thin. Ignatz thinks of a stray dog, all ribs and mange.

"Good afternoon, Miss Vargha," Ignatz says, and she looks up, blushing. He stops walking.

She returns his greeting but doesn't stop. Grimaszka pulls her leash from Ignatz's hand and chases Mara's coat. She jumps at Mara, leaving two muddy prints on her blue wool coat.

Ignatz mumbles an apology. "Bad dog!" he says to Grimaszka. "What's gotten into you?"

Mara leans down to rub at her coat. Her companion squints at Ignatz.

"Do I know you?" he says.

Ignatz extends his hand. "Dr. Ignatz von Peczely."

"The good doctor." He flashes his teeth. "Joszef Nagy," he says. His handshake is too firm. Ignatz pulls himself free, resists the temptation to wipe his hand on his trousers.

"Really, I'm sorry about my dog." Grimaszka growls. "Miss Vargha. How are you?"

"Well, the raspberries don't agree with me," she says. "I've just now gotten myself out of bed."

The man pats her arm, letting his hand linger, and Ignatz knows with certainty that Mara is pregnant. He should have thought of it sooner. He hadn't asked the right questions. He hadn't listened or paid attention.

"Come see me tomorrow morning," he says. "Early."

"So you can feed me another plant, and it will change nothing?"

"Please."

"Mara," says Joszef, taking her hand. "You should go. You can't just give up."

"I'll try," she says looking only at Joszef.

"Tomorrow, then," Ignatz says, but they are already walking away.

His desk is cluttered. He pushes everything to one side—a jar of pencils, an eraser, a small, framed photograph of his parents. There are crumpled pages he drops into the trash. He stacks the books evenly and lines them up with the edge of the desk.

Because pregnancy is a natural state for a woman, not a state of disease or brokenness, it is not reflected in the iris as Ignatz had thought it would be. He has looked for it in the eyes of many pregnant women and has located the part of the iris that represents the reproductive system: at the bottom of the iris, slightly off center. He's found that a woman's eyes are dull during her time of month, but he attributes this to a deficit of minerals in the body, minerals easily replaced once she stops bleeding.

Mara is unmarried. If he is wrong about the pregnancy she will be offended at his implications. Then again, she's been so impatient with him—maybe because it has taken him so long to recognize the nature of her problem. Is she too ashamed to bring it up herself? Does she even know? And then there is the question of her pain—pregnancy should not be so painful.

Mara's skin is so thin, so pale. Ignatz smooths the pages of his notes, turns to an empty page. There was a night once when he had thrown himself in a snowdrift and stayed there, lying on his back, letting the black sky fill his vision, watching the pinprick stars until they blurred. The snow had held him, pressing a little on all sides. His chest rising and falling. His breath drifting off in little plumes, then dissipating. He closed his eyes. He had thought, for a minute, he might sleep there. Mara: he had thought she would understand such a night, such a feeling. But she was something else.

◆◆◆

When Mara arrives, Ignatz helps her into a chair. He presses gently on her abdomen, looking for tender spots. She winces.

"There," she says.

It is the same spot, just above the hip, that he checked during her last appointment. The site of the stabbing pains. Ignatz kneads gently, the fabric of her dress coarse beneath his fingers. He smooths the fabric and presses again—finds a mass, small but almost certain. He thinks of Joszef and his bony hands, his too-firm handshake, and presses harder, watches Mara grimace.

"I've been bleeding," she offers.

"For how long?" he asks. "You should have told me."

She scowls. Her eyebrows are thick and unruly—heavy against her pale skin.

"Two weeks? On and off. I kept thinking, maybe . . ."

Ignatz busies himself with his pen, rotating it between thumb and forefinger.

"Joszef is my fiancé. . . . I guess you'd say we've sinned."

"I'm not a priest," says Ignatz, straightening up. "You're going to need surgery. You're pregnant, but the child is growing in the wrong place." Mara's face is blotchy and pink. "You can't ignore something like this."

"What sort of surgery?" she asks.

He tells her that the baby won't live, that it must be cut out.

"My father, he'll—I don't know. Can you just give me something for the pain?"

"During the surgery?"

"I can't—" she says. "I can't have surgery."

Ignatz takes her wrist. "Without it you will die."

She doesn't answer.

"I can make arrangements," Ignatz says. "Let me help you."

"Please. No. I haven't even told Joszef."

"I have a friend," Ignatz says. "He can do it. It's dangerous, but if you don't have it, you'll die. With it, you might live, though your baby will not. No matter what, this baby cannot survive. But you can."

She nods weakly and looks out the window. She presses her lips together until they turn white.

He takes her hand. "Please."

Mara Vargha, eighteen years old, complaining of lower abdominal pain. A woman: a body full of organs, each parcel in its proper place. A body: dense with fluids and tissues, loops and coils. An animal with impulses. A woman with a mind capable of controlling them.

He drops her hand.

The portion of Ignatz's diagram devoted to the heart is a miniscule splotch. The iris doesn't change color when the heart is broken. The iris does not reflect the state of the soul. It does not darken when a person tells a lie. It does not glow with love or develop a rash when a person is selfish. There is no region that reflects courage, no region that reflects lack of courage.

Ignatz sets the table for dinner with the same flowered plate he's been washing and eating from since his mother died. The same flowered plate, the same boiled cabbage, the same sausages lightly fried, the same grease lingering in the kitchen. He is setting a chipped teacup beside it when the cup slips from his hand and breaks. Grimaszka shuffles up and sniffs at the pieces. Ignatz grabs a fistful of moppy cords and pulls her away, a little roughly, and shuts her in the parlor. He sweeps the shards of the cup and kneels to push the pile into a dustpan—bits of porcelain mixed with dog hair and dust.

SHELTER

Photographs, 1975

Hand in hand on the steps of a clapboard church, Patrick and Catherine smile. She wears an A-line dress of white cotton, pearl buttons up the back, a blue sash at the waist. On her head is a wide-brimmed hat. A length of ribbon flips in the wind. Her dark hair gleams, and behind her back, Patrick tugs a greedy handful. He wears a navy suit with a polka-dot bowtie. He has long sideburns and bad teeth: cavities, football accidents, and a flight over the handlebars. Gold glints in his smile. Both are thin, and he is tall.

As the camera shutter closes and the flash explodes, Catherine's hat catches the wind and soars. Patrick laughs, so many teeth, and Catherine reaches for her hat. The other hand is on her head. Her mouth, too, is open, but wider, shrieking.

The second photo is perfect.

Splinter

First there is Daisy, a gray cat, with long, soft fur. By night she hunts the fields around their windblown farmhouse. She eats her prey at the foot of their bed. Half asleep, they hear the crunching of little bones, the rhythm of a careful tongue cleaning up after a meal. In the morning they can tell: this was a rabbit—this slick dark liver. This was a bird—this little clawed foot. Or a mouse—these tiny vertebrae.

One afternoon, Daisy brings a live rabbit into the kitchen and drops it, proudly, at Catherine's feet. It's a harmless, quivering thing, but Catherine is unsettled by its heaving sides, its flashing eyes. She considers calling Patrick at the shipyard and looks out the window at the yellow cornfield. It's nearly winter; a rabbit is a small thing. Beneath the sink she finds a pair of rubber gloves and pulls them on. She kneels and nudges the rabbit into a paper sack, which she holds at arm's length as she carries it to the edge of the cornfield. She sets it down like a flower on a grave. With her toe, she tips the bag on its side, but the rabbit doesn't come out.

A year later, a month after their first anniversary, when Catherine is pregnant, they move to a house on a dead-end road, beside a lily pond littered with sunken rowboats, home to a pair of sandhill cranes. It is quiet, hidden from wind and traffic. Patrick affixes their name to the battered mailbox and builds a split rail fence along the property line. They pour concrete for a brick patio and mark the corners with iron stakes.

It is still dark the morning Daisy jumps from the second-story balcony and lands on a stake. Patrick and Catherine are startled awake by her howls. Catherine watches from the deck while Patrick goes to her. He is afraid to lift her, afraid of causing more damage. He tries to touch her head but she tenses and snaps. Catherine calls the vet, who takes the cat, stake and all, to the clinic. As if they had shrunk from the invader, Daisy's vital organs are unharmed, but she never fully recovers. She develops oozing abscesses. She stumbles.

The Lunch Box

Every weekday morning Patrick carries his aluminum lunch box across the parking lot at work. At 7:30 a siren sounds, signaling the shift change, and the night workers pour through the gate, shaking their limbs and rubbing their eyes in the daylight. One morning, as the workers are weaving between each other, Patrick bumps a man with his lunch box, and tired and grumpy, the man shoves him. Patrick collides with the man's friend, and a fight breaks out. Patrick swings his lunch box into someone's skull, and the lunch box springs open: hardboiled egg, foil-wrapped sandwich, thermos. A paper napkin, neatly folded. The men are restrained. Patrick is suspended from work for three days.

"You could've killed someone," his supervisor says.

Patrick says, "I didn't hit him that hard."

Catherine packs his lunches in brown paper bags.

Sentinels

There are two children: Margaret, who they call Maggie, and Nora, born twenty months apart. After Nora is born, Patrick plants a blue spruce for each of his daughters, one on either side of the front door, far enough from the house that their branches and roots can extend without touching it.

Maggie is self-assured and tough, with a tangled cap of curls, not quite blonde, and quick, sturdy legs. She speaks in staccato syllables. "I'd like a ham-bur-ger," she says. "Yes. Please. I would like ketch-up." She practices throwing a foam football until the spiral is tight, no wobble. The first time it spins smoothly, she rushes to pick it up and spikes it in the grass. Maggie's face is always smudged: mud on her earlobe, dandelion yellow beneath her chin.

Nora is quiet, with dark hair and small eyes. She watches Daisy pick her way through brightly colored wooden blocks to settle in a patch of sun. She does not point. When Catherine zooms a spoonful of pureed carrots into her mouth, she opens wide, blinks, and does not laugh. No carrots ooze at the corners of her lips. Patrick grips her foot, which dangles from the high chair, between his fingers and pulls her sock until Nora kicks, and the sock slips off.

"I've got your sock," Patrick says, waving the sock, and Nora studies him, tips her head slightly, opens her mouth for more carrots.

When Nora learns to walk, she often runs in circles until she falls.

Reliable

On summer nights, when Nora is almost three, Catherine buckles her into a plastic seat on the back of her bike, and they ride along the cedar drive, away from their lily pond, past their beat-up mailbox, through the darkness to Lake Michigan. The bike tires bump over tar-patched cracks, and they watch the silver-black ribbon of water unfurl before them.

"Faster," says Nora. She hums one low note, holds it. "Look. The moon is following us."

"Mm-hm."

"Let's walk to it—like Jesus of Nazareth."

Back home, Nora finds a window from which she can wave good night to the moon. By the next week, she has to run down the driveway to see it hovering above the trees, and she waves like a pageant queen. On the night of the new moon Nora sulks, twists in the bedsheets.

Catherine sits on the edge of the bed, and Patrick stands in the doorway with a flashlight. "Look here, Nor," he says, and raises the flashlight to his mouth, stretches his lips around it, and switches it on. His cheeks glow red, taut and fibrous. He pulls the light out of his mouth to say, "I'm the man in the moon," and then puts it back and opens his eyes wide. Nora shrieks.

"Jesus, Patrick. You're scaring *me*," says Catherine, turning on the bedside lamp. "Sweetie," she says to Nora, smoothing her hair. "There are things we can't control in life, and the moon is one of them. It'll be back."

"When?"

"Soon—tomorrow. Or the next night."

"How do you know?"

"It's one of those things you can count on," Patrick says from the doorway.

"Like a best friend?"

"Well, sort of. The moon's just a rock," says Catherine. "A cold, dusty rock. It doesn't have feelings."

"A big rock," says Patrick. "The biggest."

"It glows because the sun shines on it." Catherine leans toward the lamp, and her face glows brighter. "Like this. Think of this lamp as the sun."

Nora starts to cry, and Catherine tucks her thin hair behind her ear, tries to pull her close, but she pushes her mother away. She seals herself under her quilt. Catherine sits on the edge of the bed until Nora kicks her blankets aside, plucks a shoe from the floor, and flings it at the wall.

Weeds

When the snow melts, Catherine and the girls pull fistfuls of last year's weeds from a ten-by-ten-foot garden plot. They plant peas, cabbage, carrots. They build four bamboo teepees for tomatoes and beans, but by July the garden is overtaken by white-flowering garlic mustard. Catherine spends hours weeding; the carrot greens grow spindly and pale. The mustard wraps around the bean teepees, holds tight.

Nora picks the mustard flowers and bundles them into a bouquet. Catherine snatches it and stuffs it in the burn barrel. Maggie lights the match.

Wish

Standing in the bathroom in striped boxers and socks, leaning into the mirror, Patrick finds a gray hair.

"I'm an old man," he says.

"Oh, please," says Catherine, from the bedroom. "You're a strapping young thing."

"Am I?"

"If you want to look younger you should get your teeth fixed."

He smiles too widely at his reflection. He raises one eyebrow, winks, plucks the gray strand with his thumb and forefinger.

In the bedroom, he offers the hair to Catherine in cupped hands.

"A token of my love," he says.

A puff of breath—she blows it from his hands.

Spy

Maggie, age six, lies on her belly at the edge of the pond, watching the water for tadpoles. Across the water: movement. The sandhill cranes are as tall as she is, with thin gray necks and black legs hinged with knobby knees. Their beaks are slender and sharp, their heads capped with scarlet feathers.

The smaller crane calls twice, a rattling honk, her beak uptilted. The larger one answers once, pointing his beak to the sky, and they fly, dancing like puppets, legs dangling over the water. The larger one swoops to the bank and pulls loose a tuft of grass. With his beak and a snap of his neck, he flings the grasses and they separate, alight on the surface of the pond.

"Frank," Maggie says, naming the larger bird. "And you'll be Marianne," she says to the smaller one, quietly, across the distance of the pond. The two cranes dance to exhaustion, then land together on the bank.

Once, she watches Frank fight a great blue heron for a stick. Frank loses. The heron flies off, its neck a droopy drainpipe, the stick a black slash across the pale sky. Frank stands in knee-deep water, emitting a low, wooden rattle.

She borrows Patrick's binoculars to watch the nest, waiting for the eggs to hatch. She does not invite Nora to look, though sometimes she shares her observations.

"They take turns," she tells Nora one afternoon, untying her muddy shoes in the hallway. "Sometimes Frank sits on the eggs. Sometimes Marianne."

The first egg hatches two days earlier than the second, while Maggie is at school. But she is watching when the second chick hatches and when the adult cranes leave the nest for food. The older chick repeatedly jabs the new one with its beak. Maggie does not report the death.

Cannibals

Every Sunday, at a quarter to ten, Patrick drops Catherine, Maggie, and Nora at the church playground and goes home to read the paper. The girls go to Sunday school while Catherine is in church.

At her First Communion, Maggie wears a wreath of dried baby's breath and a plain dress. She bows her head and accepts the body of Christ in cupped hands, slips the wafer into her mouth, crosses herself. Her mouth is set in a grim line. She skips the blood; Jesus sticks to the roof of her mouth, papery and dry. She scrapes him off with her tongue, kneels, and bows her head, but her eyes are flashing, wide, still looking up at boys with ties cinched at their throats. Girls in sheer veils. Hunched old women, their knotted hands curled loosely at their sides. Men in slim suits, a carnation in a buttonhole, a handkerchief in a pocket. Men in boots.

After church, Patrick drives them to a restaurant, and the girls order waffles with strawberries and whipped cream.

"Isn't it like being a cannibal?" Maggie asks.

"Don't talk with your mouth full," says Patrick. Maggie swallows.

"But isn't it?"

"It's complicated," Catherine says. She reaches across the table and wipes Nora's chin.

"Think of it as a symbol," says Patrick.

"But Sister Theodora says it's really him after the priest blesses it."

"Well, does it taste like a human body?" asks Patrick.

"It tastes like paper."

"Well, then . . ."

Maggie sets her fork down, looks Patrick in the eye.

"How would I know what a body tastes like, Dad?"

"You've eaten meat."

"Gross."

"Yeah, gross," says Nora.

"Why don't you go to church with us?" Maggie asks.

"Why don't I go to church. . . . I don't go to church because I don't believe in God."

"Patrick," says Catherine.

"She asked. You want me to lie?"

"I don't believe in God either," says Nora, her mouth full of waffles.

Nightcap

Patrick likes his whisky straight. Catherine likes a gimlet—gin. The children are sleeping. Patrick and Catherine sit on the patio in the dark, his feet in her lap. They pick green olives from a jar. Patrick licks the salt from Catherine's lips, throws his head back, calls to her like the cranes. She laughs and pushes an olive into his mouth, and he chokes. He spits the olive into his hand.

Stray

It is the morning of her first day of second grade. Maggie, wearing shorts and tube socks, is dragging a trash can to the end of the driveway. She sees a glint of orange, a hunter's arrow stuck in the side of the garage. She squints into the trees, sees nothing. She pulls the arrow out by the shaft, but the tip stays buried in the wall. She digs it out with Patrick's screwdriver. It is a streamlined, metal arrowhead, nicked and bent. She reassembles the arrow, fitting the black shaft into the tip, smoothing the plastic feathers—two orange, one yellow. She throws it once, like a dart, aiming for a tree trunk. It flies straight but strikes nothing, arcing quickly to the ground, scattering dirt. She brushes it off. She hides it beneath a stack of folded sweaters in her closet.

Sleep

Nora laughs in her sleep, so Catherine closes her door at night. In the morning, Daisy waits, sliding her paws beneath the door. During winter, Patrick goes to bed right after dinner, claiming the long hours of darkness make him tired, but he is up each day by four, drinking coffee at the kitchen table. Catherine is a fitful sleeper, often finding herself pushed to the edge of the bed with Patrick's spine pressing into her back, his cold feet touching her legs. Some nights she wakes restless and goes to the living room and sits in the dark. She listens to the pop and hiss of a record beginning to spin—then the *Cello Suites* or *The Goldberg Variations*. Maggie brushes her teeth each night at 9:15 and closes the door to her room, but often she stays up, flipping through news magazines, cutting out pictures of canyons and jungles and tattooed Maori, Inuit girls in sealskins, men in dance clubs, their faces thick with makeup. She pastes them in a notebook labeled "Travels." She builds a tent over her bed with a sheet dyed with beet juice.

Molt

Cattails blaze like flames around the pond. The cranes are gone for the winter. The grass in front of the house is tall, taller than Nora, taller than Maggie. Nora won't set foot in it, afraid of getting lost, but Maggie plunges through, forming labyrinthine tunnels, tramping a space where she lies and reads for hours.

She catches a pine snake, brown with black diamonds, twisting through the grass. Grasping it below the head, she lifts the tail with her other hand and holds it high, triumphant, the length stretched between her hands. The tip of its tail curls slowly around her wrist.

"Mom!" Maggie yells, and Catherine appears, framed by the screen door. "Come see!" Catherine pushes the door open. She is drying her hands with a checkered towel.

She laughs. "Well, look at you."

"Can I cook it?" Maggie asks. She's been reading Westerns.

"Cook it?"

"You know—on a fire."

"I don't know, Mags. That sounds messy . . . and I don't know about snakes. They might have diseases or bacteria or something. I've never heard of eating one."

"In my books they eat everything," Maggie says. "They eat rattlesnakes."

"Well, ask your father, I guess." Catherine shrugs.

When Patrick gets home from work he agrees but under the condition that Maggie kill and cut the snake herself.

Maggie carries the snake to the edge of the pond in a plastic bucket covered with a piece of cardboard. Over her shoulder she carries a spade and a crosscut saw. She spills the snake onto the ground, and Patrick steps on it with his boot as it tries to slither away, extending its head, and Maggie strikes it with the spade. She pauses after the first blow, although the snake is still alive. It pulls back, trying to coil its head into its body. Maggie has never killed anything larger than a fish. She strikes it again, twice, and it stops moving. She saws its head off while Patrick goes inside to wash his hands, although he has not touched anything.

By the time Patrick returns she has sliced along the snake's belly and is removing the skin with deft tugs. Patrick gathers deadwood. Maggie cooks chunks of meat on a skewer over a fire. It blackens quickly, without sizzle or pop.

Seated at the picnic table, Maggie offers her plate to Nora, who takes a delicate bite and chews carefully before pushing it back to Maggie, who laughs and finishes the rest.

"Next, I want to try possum," Maggie says.

Catherine shakes her head. "Whose kid are you?"

Scolds

A pie on the counter, crust nibbled away. Maggie's new blue jeans in the hamper with a torn knee. A dead bird, wrapped neatly in tissue, stashed in Nora's patent leather shoe. Over and over, the screen door snaps on its hinges, bangs closed. A penguin drawn on the steamed window of the Buick shows up ghostly every time the windows fog. A tin of tobacco nests in Patrick's jacket pocket. Water boils away on the stove, gray smoke, a burned-black pot. Maggie misses the bus, walks home from school singing, alone. Nora watches *Jaws* on late-night TV—nightmares give her away. A missed pill, a missed period. Sour milk pushed to the back of the fridge, curds running down the drain. A miscarriage, and Catherine curls in a dark room, her secret spoiled.

Percussion

At dinner Nora clinks her fork against her glass.

"Kiss. Kiss," she orders her parents.

Catherine takes the fork away, says, "Eat your potatoes."

Roller Rink

A door in Patrick and Catherine's bedroom leads to the unfinished loft full of boxes and wrapping paper, window fans, an old bicycle, an American flag neatly folded. The walls are naked insulation, pink fiberglass, which Maggie and Nora learn not to touch but not until Nora has developed a rash up the back of one leg. The floors are yellow particleboard, and the room seems to glow and hold its breath. The girls bring their father's shop radio from the garage and push the boxes against one wall. They circle in their roller skates.

"Reverse skate!" Maggie announces, and they switch direction.

They set up a limbo game with a yardstick and boxes but find it is too difficult to lower the stick, almost impossible to find and position enough evenly-sized boxes while wearing skates. They give up.

At the back of the loft, there is a pair of doors that, when opened, look onto the lily pond. If the loft were finished, these doors would exit to a balcony or stairway, but as it is, they open into hazy, green air, dust suspended in sunlight, occasional blowing leaves. The girls are forbidden to open these doors, but when they know their mother is in the kitchen, their father at work, they swing the doors open and sit in the doorway, skates dangling. They throw things: loose nails, chewing gum, an apple core.

Looker

Catherine is planting irises around the mailbox while Nora and Maggie play Go-Fish in the grass. She wears a sunhat and a bright pink bathing suit, her bare shoulders tanned and freckled. From a passing car, a whistle.

"Woo, Mom," says Maggie. "Maybe you better put on a shirt."

"Why should I?" Catherine says.

"You're a married woman," says Maggie.

"So? It's nice to get some attention once in a while. And anyway, I'm in my own yard."

"Shouldn't you get your attention from Dad?" says Nora. Catherine packs the dirt tight around a bulb and straightens.

"Well, I do, but married women like to know they've still got what it takes." She smiles and wipes the sweat from her temple with the back of her hand.

Residue

Patrick's sweat smells like raisins. Shaking out his tee shirts in the laundry room, Catherine smells it—sleepy, rich, a little sour. The smell is in the bedsheets. And in his shoes, right after he takes them off.

"Raisins," she says, when he is undressing at night, and he throws his tee shirt at her. She throws it back, says, "If you ever die, the sight of oatmeal on the stove will make me cry."

He lies down and she bites his shoulder. She bites her own lip, hard, draws blood. Patrick pulls her close.

Comet

The winter the comet is in the sky Patrick says, "Once every seventy-six years, girls. A once-in-a-lifetime chance, girls. Next time it's visible, you'll be old women. Blind, probably. And I'll be dead."

He takes the girls to a beach early in the morning. Six inches of crusty snow push up Nora's pants and scrape her skin. Patrick stands between his daughters, binoculars raised to the black sky. He knows from his star charts where the comet should be, but he cannot find it. The girls each take a turn with the binoculars but see only bright, jumbled stars, black. Even snug in their boots, their toes begin to hurt, then tingle and buzz. Along the surface of the lake, the sky grows blue and they walk to the car.

Two weeks later, Patrick is sitting in the backyard, drinking beer from a bottle, when he sees it. He calls them, but Catherine is washing dishes. The girls shiver in nightgowns and boots.

"That's it?" says Maggie, following Patrick's finger. "That?"

"Mom!" Nora calls. "Come out."

The three stand, watching the sky. Finally, they hear the door open behind them and Catherine joins them.

"So you found it," she says. Patrick hooks an arm loosely around her neck.

"We found it," he says.

"Is it all it's cracked up to be?" Catherine says, squinting.

"Yes," says Nora.

"No," say Patrick and Maggie.

"What did you expect?" Nora says, but no one answers. Nora blows the comet a kiss. "You're splendid, darling," she says. "Grand." To her family she says, "It's old, that comet."

The comet looks like an icy thumbprint—a tiny, dusty smudge.

Surprise

Maggie hides behind the bathroom door, feeling her heart beat in her throat. She makes certain her toes are not peeking, her shadow is not stretched across the floor. Her shoulder blades press against the wall behind her. She tries to silence her breathing. Patrick's boots clomp in the hallway. She waits, watches for his silhouette beneath the door. His hand is on the doorknob.

Maggie jumps out, shouts, "HA!"

Patrick grabs her forearm.

"Don't ever. Do that. Again."

Later, Patrick knocks on Maggie's door. She doesn't answer. He knocks again, pushes the door open, slowly. "Hey," he says. "I'm sorry." She doesn't look at him.

At dinner he makes a new rule: no jumping out, no surprises.

Portraits

In her second-grade school picture, Maggie wears the faux beavertail hat Patrick bought her at Frontierland. At first, Catherine refuses to hang the portrait in the hall, next to Nora's kindergarten picture. In her third-grade picture, Maggie is missing three teeth and laughs with an open mouth. In fourth grade, a half hour before the class lines up for individual photos, Maggie excuses herself to the bathroom, where she cuts off her shoulder-length curls with plastic-handled scissors. She leaves her hair in the sink. In the fifth grade, she wears a fuzzy pink sweater and pink lipstick. She stuffs her training bra. She cocks her head slightly to the side, smiles with half her mouth, flutters her eyelids lazily.

Cinema

Catherine closes her eyes and leans back on the sofa. A cello trills and sustains. Nora, barefoot, stands in the doorway.

"Mom," Nora whispers. "Mom, what are you doing?"

"You're up early," Catherine says, straightening up. "I'm listening to a record."

"Are you sad?" Nora asks.

"No. I'm not sad." Catherine pats the cushion next to her. "Come here." Nora crosses the room and sits down. "Close your eyes. I like to make up a movie that only I can see. A movie that goes with the music." Catherine closes her eyes. Nora watches her.

"What's happening?" Nora asks.

After a minute Catherine answers. "An ice skater with a long scarf. It's snowing a little and she's going somewhere, skating across a lake. I can see her breath."

Nora closes her eyes.

Chernobyl

Televised voices twist up the stairs to Nora, lying on her back in the dark, and to Maggie, huddled with a flashlight and a magazine. For hours, the voices drone on, their low cant broken only by the electronic blips and scales of news music. At breakfast, Catherine's hair is ragged and uncombed. Maggie and Nora usually take the bus to school, but today, Catherine drives them.

When she picks them up, Nora sits in the back. Maggie throws her backpack in first, sits shotgun, rolls down the window. She puts her hand out into the bold sun.

"Dirk Nelson says a poison cloud is coming from Russia. He says it will kill us or make us grow an extra head," she says.

"Roll your window up, please," Catherine says. "It isn't that warm."

Maggie pulls her hand in but leaves the window down. "Dirk said he saw it on the news—that the president said so."

Catherine covers her face with one hand, rubs her eyes, exhales. "Dirk Nelson's wrong."

"But the *president* said."

"There was an accident in Russia, an explosion," says Catherine. "No one knows what will happen, but Russia is far, far away from here. You won't grow an extra head."

"But we could die?"

"You won't die."

"How do you know?"

"It's very far away. The cloud will fall apart before it gets here. People did die, though. People there died. People in Russia. And more of them will get sick and probably die."

"Babies?" asks Nora.

"Yes, babies. Babies. Mothers. Fathers. Everyone."

"But—"

"Mags, I don't want to talk about this."

"Can I watch the news?" asks Maggie.

"No. Roll up your window."

Smooth

In the shower, Maggie cuts her shin with Catherine's razor. The cut grows white, then bleeds, five inches long. Blood braids with water; Maggie turns the shower off. She tamps the cut with toilet paper, but when she pulls the paper off, the wound reopens. She fills the trash can, crumples clean tissues on top. She sticks band-aids horizontally across the cut, eight of them, and ties a bandanna tight around her leg. She wears sweatpants, rinses the razor, sets it in her parents' shower, behind the bottle of shampoo. The uncut leg she shows to Nora, sliding her pants leg up to her knee.

"You look like a plucked chicken," Nora says.

"Well, plucked chickens are sexier than feathery ones," Maggie says.

Drowner

Nora draws on the front step with a chunk of sandstone. A jack-o-lantern. A brontosaurus with leaves hanging from its mouth. She writes GIRAFFE and draws one with excessively knobby knees. A candle with a tear-shaped flame and a halo. A many-windowed building burning. A girl in a skirt, beneath jagged waves, bubbles in a vertical line from her open mouth. She draws a thought cloud, fills it with the word FUCK.

She is sent to her room without dinner. All weekend she rakes leaves into piles. Maggie jumps in them. Nora rakes again. She washes dishes, cleans the refrigerator.

The yellow sandstone washes away, but pale scratches remain.

Pure

Catherine is out grocery shopping when the salesman makes his way up the walk and between the sentinel spruces, now ten feet tall. Maggie answers the door but leaves the screen latched.

"Your mother home, little lady?" the salesman asks. He wears a brown felt hat and loafers with fringe. His face is ruddy and slightly pocked, but his nose is straight and his brown eyes clear and wide-set.

"Nope."

"How 'bout your father?"

"Nope."

"You have a grandma hiding in there?" He leans in, looking over Maggie's head, into the house.

"No," Maggie says, standing straighter.

"Well, can I leave these with you?" The man fans out an assortment of brochures.

"No."

"They're about drinking water. You just can't over-purify your water these days. I'll leave them here on the step. You tell your mom they're here," he says, bending to set the brochures down. Maggie opens the screen door into his head. He stumbles back.

"Hey," he says, catching himself. The door snaps shut. Maggie presses her body into the screen and glares.

"Hey," she says.

He walks back down the walk, straightening his hat. He looks over his shoulder, and Maggie sticks out her tongue.

Inventory

In the trampled grass near the pond, Patrick finds a can of beer, unopened, and a cigar box in a plastic bag; a round, pink stone; a Robin Yount baseball card; two wrapped tampons; a cigarette; a crane's feather; a fork with its stem broken and sharpened, tines bent for gripping, extended at skewed angles.

Maggie is sweeping the garage.

"What is this?" He holds the weapon up, the cigar box tucked beneath the other arm.

"That's my stuff," Maggie says, reaching for the box, but he shakes the fork at her.

"Where did you get this?"

Maggie narrows her eyes.

"This is a weapon, Maggie." He dumps the contents of the cigar box on the floor and grinds the pile under his boot. "You're grounded."

"I found it," Maggie says. "At school."

"You're still grounded." He backs out of the garage, clutching the fork, his knuckles white.

Crush

In the middle of the night, a week before Maggie's twelfth birthday, two high school boys turn onto the dead-end road and pass the beat-up mailbox without noticing. They tear along the drive, around the final curve toward the house. In the backseat is a half-empty case of beer, a pair of fishing rods, a flashlight, waders. They drive through a low cluster of junipers, uprooting them, and through the wall of Maggie's bedroom. The house shudders.

The car pushes Maggie's bed into her closet. Maggie sits up screaming. Patrick throws open her bedroom door, stands with his feet planted, his nakedness illuminated by the cockeyed headlights. Plaster and glass are falling, tinkling. The air is hazy with dust, tangy with juniper. He looks across the smoking car, through the torn wall, into the night. He looks at Maggie and picks her up, lifts her from her bed. He carries her from the room where, already, the dust is settling. The dust is falling like snow.

Departure

Catherine carries Daisy to the far side of the pond. The cat is too light; Catherine feels her knobby ribs through her fur. She sets her at the edge of the knee-high grass. She runs a finger along the cat's throat, scratches her threadbare ears, slides her hand over Daisy's bony hips, follows her tail to the tip, releases it. Daisy steps into the grass. Lopsided, she picks her way through the field.

"A zillion mice," Catherine whispers.

AUTHOR'S NOTE

Much of my fiction is informed and inspired by research and by historical images gathered from junk shops, libraries, books, ephemera dealers, garage sales, and the wormholes of the internet. I owe a great debt to the writers and artists, named or anonymous, whose work has fed my own. A few of my sources for the stories in this collection are listed below.

The images and italicized text in "Real Silk" are taken from a set of pamphlets published by Real Silk Hosiery Mills of Indiana in 1923.

The image that accompanies "The Mugged Body," is from Geoffroy Tory's book *Champ Fleury*, published in 1529. Tory was a French engraver, typographer, and author with an idiosyncratic theory regarding fonts and the relation of letters to the human form. He is best known for introducing the apostrophe, accents, and the cedilla into the printing of the French language.

"Until We See Signs and Wonders" was inspired and informed by Sidney D. Kirkpatrick's *Edgar Cayce: An American Prophet* (Riverhead Books, 2000).

"We Are a Teeming Wilderness" was sparked by Michael Pollan's 2013 article in *The New York Times Magazine* titled "Some of My Best Friends Are Germs."

ACKNOWLEDGMENTS

Short stories were my first love as a writer. They remain one of my favorite genres to read and to write because I find that they especially invite experimentation in form and voice. I wrote the stories in this collection across a span of many years, so this book is a record of my shifting fascinations and the many delightful rabbit holes in which I found myself. Thank you to the friends and family who inspired these stories, sometimes by sharing their own stories and obsessions with me, and to the writers and editors who helped make them better stories.

My professors in the MFA program at Washington University—Kellie Wells, Kathryn Davis, and Marshall Klimasewiski—read the earliest of these stories as if they mattered, and so I began to believe that they could. My professors at the University of Utah, especially Melanie Rae Thon, Lance Olsen, and Paisley Rekdal, provoked wildness in my writing and thinking, some of which has made it into these pages. My MFA cohort at Wash U and my PhD cohort at the University of Utah shaped these stories—and my life—immeasurably. I am especially grateful to Anton DiSclafani, TaraShea Nesbit, Robert Glick, Rachel Marston, and Raphael Dagold for our ongoing exchanges of stories and essays, and even more for their friendship. My colleagues and students at Earlham College and Cornell College, especially Glenn Freeman, Rebecca Entel, and Rachel Swearingen, are an important part of the writer I am today. To my current colleagues at Union College, thank you for being a stable and encouraging community in which to write and teach.

For their help with this book, I am especially grateful to Jordan Smith, Judith Lewin, and Debbie Catharine. Thank you to Claire Foxx for choosing this collection as the winner of the 2022 Press 53 Prize for Short Fiction, and for her tireless editing and beautiful cover design, and thank you to Kevin Morgan Watson and Press 53 for publishing this book, and for providing one more essential avenue along which short stories can make their way out into the world in books.

I have been told it is frowned upon to dedicate a book to a pet, but my cat Lucy was with me from the time I wrote the first of these stories until I had completed the last. I unknowingly named her after the patron saint of writers, and for years she offered the steadiest gaze and affection, no matter how the writing was going.

Thank you, always, to my parents for insisting that I do what I loved, even when it was impractical advice, and thank you to Jesse for putting up with it all.

♦♦♦

The author would also like to thank the editors and literary magazines that first published these stories, sometimes in slightly different forms:

Alaska Quarterly Review, "Two Birds"

Black Warrior Review, "Anatomy of the Eye"

Conjunctions, "Benevolence"

Geist, "The Course to the Horizon"

Land Grant College Review, "Shelter"

Matchbook, "Dispatches from Abandoned Architecture"

Miracle Monocle, "The Other Matter"

Pacifica, "We Are a Teeming Wilderness"

PANK, "Papyrus of the Yellow-Throated Warbler"

Southern Humanities Review, "Until We See Signs & Wonders"

Sou'wester, "This Precarious Hive"

The Tusculum Review, "Real Silk"

Versal, "The Mugged Body"

Shena McAuliffe is the author of *The Good Echo: A Novel* (Black Lawrence Press, 2018), and *Glass, Light, Electricity: Essays* (University of Alaska, 2020). Her short stories and essays have been widely published, and she holds a PhD in Literature and Creative Writing from the University of Utah and an MFA in Fiction Writing from Washington University in St. Louis. She grew up in Wisconsin and Colorado and now lives in Schenectady, New York, where she is the John D. and Catherine T. MacArthur Assistant Professor of English at Union College.

Printed in the USA
CPSIA information can be obtained
at www.ICGtesting.com
LVHW040324150823
755207LV00004B/458